RETURN OF THE RUNAWAY BRIDE

RETURN OF THE RUNAWAY BRIDE

DONNA FASANO

Find Donna Fasano on the web:
Her blog: DonnaFasano.com
On Facebook: Facebook.com/DonnaFasanoAuthor
On Twitter: Twitter.com/DonnaFaz
On Pinterest: Pinterest.com/DonnaFaz

Contents

What reviewers are saying about Return of the Runaway Bride:

"So what did I think about these characters? Spot-on!"
~Misty Baker, A KindleObsessed Review

"I highly recommend this book if you are looking for a sweet and realistic love story."
~The Autumn Review, Book Review Blogger

"Ms. Fasano's ability to throw humor into her writing adds richness to the story, and had me laughing many times. Fantastic book!"
~Allie-Kat, Amazon Kindle Customer

PROLOGUE

———————

"I need to slip down to the kitchen to check with the caterer. I'll be right back to pin on your veil. I won't be two minutes, promise." The woman hesitated at the door and gazed warmly at her daughter. Sudden emotion glistened in her eyes. "Oh, honey, you're going to make a beautiful bride."

Savanna Langford watched the door of her bedroom close as her mother bustled out and then she took a deep, calming breath. Sitting down on the very edge of her bed so as not to crease the delicate double galloon lace covering her wedding gown, Savanna looked around the room that had sheltered both her and her dreams for all nineteen years of her life.

The pale-green spread covering the bed was sumptuous and soft. The matching curtains ruffling in the gentle breeze allowed the perfect amount of sunlight to shine through the open window. White bookshelves held all the classic novels that should be read by a proper young woman. Everything surrounding her was neat, tidy, pristine. This was a perfect room, in a perfect house, where she'd spent her perfect youth growing up in a perfect world.

And now the next phase of her life was soon to unfold before her. She was about to take part in the perfect wedding and marry the perfect man.

That Daniel Walsh III was the perfect man was no secret. Everyone said so. Danny was loving, caring, kind and gentle. Not only that, but Miz Ida, owner of Watson's Kwik-E Mart, adamantly declared that he was the most handsome man in the county. And Savanna's father had boasted on more than one occasion that Danny would be an excellent provider once he finished his final year of law school and passed the bar. Yes, everyone agreed that Danny Walsh was the best catch in town.

Savanna tipped her chin high and stared at the ceiling. "So what's wrong with me?" she murmured. She knew Danny was perfect, that was one reason why she loved him with all her heart and soul. She'd never met another man like him.

Why, then, when she was about to embark on a lifelong journey with the man of her dreams, was she plagued with such doubt? Why, on what should be the happiest day of her life, did she feel as if she were being followed by an ominous thunder cloud?

There was no denying the dark cloud. It had been hanging over her head now for two full weeks.

She stood and paced the length of the room, twisting the fingers of both hands together this way and that.

"It's *nerves*," she said in a firm, loud voice. "It's only nerves. Put it out of your head."

Pressing a fist against her solar plexus, Savanna forced the tension from her trembling stomach and the distressing questions from her mind.

"Here I am." Savanna's mother rushed into the

room, stopped and flattened her palm against her chest. "Oh, my. I need to slow down and take a breath."

A tender smile pulled at Savanna's mouth at the sight of her mother. "I know how hard you're working to make this a wonderful day for me, Mom," she said.

It was so like her mother to overwork herself. Each and every birthday was made special, each holiday an elaborate affair, because Mrs. Langford fussed to make everything perfect for her husband and only child.

Savanna's mother dismissed the compliment with a wave. "It's what being a mother is all about, honey. Now come. Sit." She patted the cushioned chair facing the mirrored vanity and fluffed the skirt of Savanna's gown after her daughter sat down.

"You should see Danny." The woman's blue eyes twinkled. "He looks so handsome in his tux. That black suit brings out the best of his dark good looks." Smoothing her hand along one side of Savanna's blond, upswept hair, she commented, "It's a shame your friends couldn't be here for the wedding."

"Maggie and Sharon left for school two weeks ago," Savanna said, a flash of sadness rushing through her at the thought of her friends who were now on the other side of the country. "And Josie was lucky to get an internship at that pharmaceutical company. With everyone just getting settled, it was too much to ask them to fly home again."

Mrs. Langford cocked a wicked eyebrow at her daughter's reflection. "Well, if they could see Danny today, they'd simply swoon."

Savanna laughed. "Swoon? Mom, no one 'swoons' anymore."

"Oh, yes, they do." Her lips quirked in a perky smile. "They just call it something else."

Savanna thought her mother was probably right; if her friends had been sitting downstairs, they most likely would have been swooning at the sight of Danny in a tux. But then the sight of Danny, no matter what his attire, had driven her high school friends crazy ever since he'd first shown an interest in Savanna. Maggie would consistently turn three shades of red, and Sharon would giggle herself silly. Josie, on the other hand, had always been pea green with envy because Savanna was involved with a "college man."

And now those same friends she'd graduated with were off seeking their destinies at colleges and corporations across the country. A small frown creased her brow as the black cloud of doubt billowed and thickened and hovered closer than ever.

"Oh, I forgot to tell you. Danny's parents arrived while I was downstairs." Savanna's mother gently shook out the folds of the gossamer veil. "They're with your father. I've never seen Daniel and Susan happier. And your father's floating around down there with a smile on his face that's a mile wide."

As she watched the reflection of her mother arranging the white, lacy panels of French silk tulle over her head, Savanna struggled to breathe. She supposed this match between herself and Danny had been a given from the very beginning...to her friends, her parents, Danny's family, even to Danny himself. And that had never bothered her before. So why did she find the thought so claustrophobic now?

Mrs. Langford positioned the stiff, satin-covered

band on her daughter's head and began to pin it securely in place.

"You're going to make a wonderful wife," she said. "And your father and I can't wait to be grandparents."

But Savanna wasn't listening; she was concentrating on sorting out the feelings churning inside her.

Danny's attentions had always flattered her, had always made her feel special. His touch excited her, his kisses made her tremble. Being with him, she felt protected and secure. Danny would keep her safe, just as safe as she'd always been here at home, living with her parents.

As if she were a mind reader, Mrs. Langford said, "After today you'll have no worries." Her mother chattered on, not noticing Savanna's silence. "As the wife of a lawyer, your future will be set. I can't find the words to express just how happy I am. This is what your dad and I always planned for you."

As the words echoed in her head, Savanna's mind reeled. Her eyes widened a fraction as a realization struck her with force—everything had been planned for her. Every single aspect of her life had been mapped out by those who loved her.

She'd always been sheltered, kept perfectly safe from the outside world. Never had she been touched by unpleasantness of any kind, never had she faced a problem alone.

Savanna struggled to remember one time in all her nineteen years when she had encountered and tackled an obstacle on her own, one time when she had overcome a challenge single-handed. The fact that she couldn't recall even one instance was mind-boggling.

"Mother..." Savanna's voice was raspy with dry emotion. "I can't do this."

Mrs. Langford continued to fuss with the headpiece. "Can't do what, honey?" she asked blithely.

"I can't marry Danny."

"Of course you can." For several seconds, Mrs. Langford kept pinning the delicate veiling material, but Savanna's prolonged silence made her glance up. After studying her daughter's expression, she must have read the panic there, for her tone changed dramatically as she straightened and asked, "What do you mean you can't marry Danny?"

Savanna squeezed her eyes shut. "I don't know

what I mean. It's hard to put in to words. I'm feeling something, and I'm not sure what it is." Her eyes were pleading for understanding when she looked up. "Something just isn't right."

"Don't be silly," her mother reproved. "You love Danny."

Twisting around to face her mother, Savanna said, "Of course I love him. He's wonderful."

"He is," her mother agreed, her voice suddenly tight. "And he'll take care of you. It's what your father and I want for you. It's what everyone wants for you, Savanna."

But was that what she wanted for herself? For someone to care for her for the rest of her days? The questions whirled inside her head, and Savanna was surprised by the tears that prickled her eyelids.

By marrying Danny was she merely fulfilling everyone else's expectations of what was best for her? If she did marry him, how would she ever know what she, Savanna Langford, was capable of achieving? How would she know what challenges might be awaiting her out in the world?

Who am I? she wondered. What do I want for myself? The questions rocked her to her very foundation. She had never asked that of herself before.

She might not know the answers to any of the questions that were rearing up in her mind, but she did know that she couldn't possibly commit herself to Danny until she had the chance to at least ponder them.

Immediately she reached up and began pulling at the pins that held the headpiece in place.

"Savanna, stop that," her mother demanded.

The two of them engaged in what would have been a comical bout, as one plucked out hairpins and the other tried to snatch the pins and put them back into place. But there was nothing funny about the despair pushing Savanna to the brink of hysteria.

"Mother!" Frustrated by the game, Savanna stood so quickly the chair toppled over.

Mrs. Langford scowled. "You're being silly, Savanna. This is nothing but an attack of pre-wedding jitters." She stooped down and picked up the pins that had fallen to the floor. "It's usually the groom who gets cold feet."

"I cannot do this." Savanna's unflinching gaze made it evident that she was utterly serious.

Mrs. Langford stood and planted her hands on her trim hips. "The minister has arrived. The guests are assembled. Everyone is waiting for the bride's entrance." She cocked her head. "The bride is *you*, Savanna."

Savanna swallowed and tipped up her chin a fraction. "I need to talk to Danny."

Mrs. Langford's lips pursed so tightly that they paled under her sheer lipstick. After a long, tense moment, she said, "All right. I'll go find him. I only hope he can talk some sense into you."

After the door closed firmly, leaving her alone with her doubts and questions, Savanna wondered what on earth she was going to say to Danny. How could she explain her feelings? How could she make him understand when she didn't understand herself?

Fear and confusion gripped her with an icy hand and she buried her face in her open palms. "What are you doing?" she murmured.

There was a soft knock at the door. "Savanna?"

A familiar warmth rippled through her at the sound of Danny's deep, rich voice.

"Danny!" Her urgent whisper was nearly choked off by a sob as she pulled open the door.

The very sight of him calmed her and she drank in the comfort his presence never failed to give. The smile that tilted his lips gave her strength and she tried valiantly to return a smile of her own.

"You're beautiful," he said. "But with all the superstition about bad luck, are you sure it's safe for me to see you before the ceremony?"

His jesting tone told her that he didn't realize the extent of her emotional state. Maybe it was better that he didn't know the turmoil she was feeling. What she needed to do was explain to him in clear, logical terms the chaos that was twisting around in her brain. The contradiction in terms nearly made her laugh aloud. Instead she took a deep breath.

"Danny," she began. It hurt to say his name, knowing what she was about to tell him. "I'm afraid I can't do this."

He took her hands in his and held them securely. The feel of his skin on hers was stirring. All she wanted to do was drift deeper into his protective embrace. No, her mind screamed. Not now.

"Savanna, everything's going to be all right. You'll see, as soon as we..."

His voice trailed off as she began to shake her head. She pulled her hands from his grasp and stepped back. She couldn't touch him and think clearly at the same time.

"You don't understand," she said. "I'm afraid."

"I know you are."

She saw his dark eyes fill with compassion and love.

God, why can't I get this right? 'Afraid' wasn't the word she'd meant to say. Anxiety swept through her, settling in the pit of her stomach where it churned, slowly and steadily.

"Listen," he said, "I'll go down and tell everyone that we need some time." He reached out and gently cupped her elbow. "Say, an hour? That will give us time to talk." He chuckled. "Time for us to gather up your courage."

"But-"

"It's okay," he told her. "Dad can break open the champagne early. There'll be no harm in that, now will there?" He gave her a charming, lopsided grin.

Hope budded like a rose inside Savanna. Looking at Danny so confident and assured, she wondered how she had ever doubted that he couldn't make everything right.

He went over and uprighted the chair, leading her with him. "Now you sit down and relax." He settled her in the seat, leaned close and caressed her cheek with his strong, smooth fingers. "It's going to be all right, Savanna. I promise."

His lips were warm and moist as he pressed them against hers. "I'll be right back with a glass of bubbly." He grinned. "And then I'll remind you of all those dreams we made. That'll ease your nerves." He kissed her softly on the mouth.

When Savanna was alone she sat in the warm cocoon of security in which Danny had left her wrapped. She didn't need to worry. Everything was going to be just fine, perfect even.

Those two tiny words sent an icy prickle chasing up her spine. The shadowy cloud of apprehension that descended was thick enough to smother her.

"Oh, God!" The words ripped from her throat like a torturing claw as she ran toward her closet and wrenched out the suitcase she'd so carefully packed for her two week honeymoon.

She snatched the bridal veil from her head, barely wincing as the pins snagged then pulled free from her hair. She reached behind her to rip at the back of her gown, and a dozen dainty pearl buttons bounced soundlessly on the plush carpet.

CHAPTER ONE

───────

Six years later

Welcome to Fulton, Virginia. The wooden sign was weathered, but the letters were bright with fresh paint. Savanna had been in high school when the town council had voted to create the quaint welcome area with its cheery greeting and evergreen shrubs. She remembered that the Ladies' Auxiliary had always been responsible for manicuring the mound, and the crimson begonias and deep purple petunias were proof that the Ladies were still taking the job seriously.

As she crossed the town limit, Savanna released

one hand from the steering wheel and reached up to massage her neck. Ever since she'd decided to return to her hometown, trepidation had coiled inside her tighter and tighter. It had been six years since she'd left behind everything important in her life, her friends, her family, the man she loved.

"No," she murmured, refusing to dwell on unpleasant thoughts. There would be plenty of time to deal with all that. In fact, that's exactly why she had returned to Fulton. But for the moment, Savanna wanted to enjoy her homecoming, savor the sights and sounds of the town in which she'd spent her youth. The place she'd missed so desperately.

As she passed familiar scenes, the Bowl-A-Rama, Garvy's Service Station and Bob's Barber Shop with its red-and-white swirled column still spinning, the long years melted away until it could have been just yesterday that she'd driven out of town as if the hounds of hell were on her scent.

Savanna stopped at the red light and closed her eyes. She shivered in spite of the warm, southern sun as icy doubt brought cold, realistic questions. Would the folks in town be happy to see her? Would they welcome her with open arms? Or turn their backs on her because of "the big scandal," as Savanna had come to name that episode of her life? The older residents worried her most, the ones whose memories were sure to be razor sharp and as clear as the lenses in their reading glasses.

And how would Daniel and Susan Walsh respond to her return? Would they see her long enough for her to explain her reasons for running away from marrying their son? They had to, Savanna thought. They simply had to.

Danny flashed into her mind and a band of apprehension tightened across her chest. How on earth was she ever going to face him? How was she going to make him understand what...

"Please stop." She spoke the words loud and clear. All these questions would drive her insane. Take one problem at a time, Savanna, she told herself.

She crossed the intersection and caught sight of Watson's Kwik-E Mart. "E for efficient. E for economical. And don't forget Kwik." Mr. Watson had come up with the marketing campaign all on his own, and he'd kept a copy of the neatly cut-out newspaper ad tacked behind the checkout counter.

On impulse, Savanna made a sharp left into the

parking lot and turned off the car's engine. The lesson of facing her problems head-on was one Savanna had learned quickly after leaving Fulton. If she wanted answers to her anxious questions...

"There's no better time to find out than right now," she said. She got out of her car and walked toward the shop's entrance. Inhaling deeply, she thrust back her shoulders and pushed open the glass door.

Miz Ida, as all the neighborhood children had called the spirited, energetic woman, was busy at the counter with a customer. Savanna picked up a plastic basket and began scanning the shelves of groceries.

She put a box of tea bags in the basket and glanced toward the counter. Savanna fondly recalled Ida Watson as the town gossip, the one person who knew everything about everyone.

Would the woman even recognize her? Savanna wondered. Or would she be forced to go through the embarrassing task of introducing herself? Don't be silly, she chided. Of course Miz Ida would remember her. Hadn't she slipped Savanna about a million cinnamon jawbreakers over the years? Besides, Savanna's mother was certain to have told

Miz Ida of her daughter's impending return. And if Ida knew, then probably everyone in town knew too.

Actually, Savanna hoped to glean from Ida some impression of how others in town would greet her. If anyone could tell her what to expect, Miz Ida could.

Ida's gossip, so far as Savanna could remember, had never been malicious, simply matter-of-fact. And the woman's softhearted nature might compel her to keep the sticky questions concerning Savanna's past to a minimum.

Ha, I should be so lucky, Savanna thought as she chose a quart container of skim milk and tucked it in her basket beside a small brick of cheddar cheese.

"Savanna?" The voice behind her was uncertain.

Startled, Savanna turned. And then she smiled.

"Savanna Langford!" Ida threw her wiry arms around Savanna and gave her a warm hug. "It's so good to see you. You look lovely. Just lovely."

"Well, thank you, Miz Ida," Savanna said. "You look wonderful too."

"Fit as a fiddle, I'm happy to say." Ida's eyes glittered with pride. "I don't suffer from bursitis, arthritis or any of those old-fogey ailments. I'm so healthy, this store's been open every day but Christmas for the past twenty-three years." Ida chuckled. "Oh, I did close down one Saturday last year for Chrissy's wedding."

"Your daughter got married?" Savanna asked.

"Finally did it. Caught herself a pharmacist from Richmond. I hated to see her move away, but she's happy as a bear cub in a honey factory and that's all that counts." Ida took the plastic basket from Savanna, moved up the short aisle and set it on the counter. "But enough about me and mine. I want to hear all about you."

"Well," Savanna said. "I'm back."

"I can sure see that. I was right happy to hear that you bought the house when your parents retired south. I hated to see them go, but you know how they longed for that sunny climate." Ida shook her head. "I don't see how they stand all that heat, myself. But your mother called me last week, and she was just bubbling. Told me all about how you'd be comin' this week." Planting a fist on her hip, Ida continued, "Like I said, I'm glad you bought the house. It would have been awful to see it go to strangers."

Savanna shoved aside the clamor of emotions that careered inside her at the thought of strangers owning her childhood home. "It's a good investment." She nodded emphatically as she said the words.

Ida's eyebrows lifted a fraction. "An investment?"

"Um-hmm. I plan to renovate the house and rent it out." She shrugged. "I may stay in Fulton a few weeks, a month maybe, while I do some fixing up, but then I have to go back to Baltimore."

"Oh." Ida's voice held a note of bewilderment. After a moment of silence, she blurted, "I sure am glad you and your ma are back on speaking terms." Her voice lowered to a murmur as she said, "For a long while there, every time your name was mentioned your ma's mouth would pucker up like she was sucking a lemon."

Savanna shrugged an admission. "Mom was pretty upset about my... leaving Fulton the way I did."

Ida pursed her lips and whistled. "Upset is putting it mildly, honey. She was fuming. Mad as the proverbial wet hen, she was." Then her face became serious. "She finally got over it, though."

"Yes, she finally did. I can't tell you the number of letters she returned to me unopened. Or the number of times she hung up the phone just hearing my voice on the other end."

Ida's eyes softened. "That must have hurt, child."

"Well," Savanna said, "she was..." Her voice trailed as she shook her head.

"I know, angry. And embarrassed." Ida's chin dipped as she commented, "And there wasn't another person in Fulton who could hold a grudge like Margaret Langford. Remember that time when Les Richards let his pooch go doodie in your mother's flower beds? Lordy, she was fit to be tied." Ida's eyes danced at the humorous memory. "She never did speak to that man again. And she tried to douse that dog with the water hose every time he came anywhere near her yard." Ida hooted with laughter.

"I was never allowed to play with Rags again," Savanna added. "It was awful because I loved that pup." The disconcerting memory wasn't enough to keep her from joining in with Ida's amusement.

"Your mother was one stubborn woman," Ida commented.

"It wasn't all her fault that it took months to straighten things out between us," Savanna had to admit. "For a while she didn't even know where I was."

"Well," Ida said, her tone making the word light and airy, "that's certainly understandable. You needed time to sort things out for yourself."

The empathy in Ida's eyes pulled at Savanna to elaborate. But before she could speak, warning bells jangled in her head, signals that were a reminder of Ida's gossipy nature. Savanna had come into the store seeking information about public opinion concerning herself, not to disclose some tidbit that would start stories flying like a flock of squawking crows. She was certain there would be enough of that without her help.

When Savanna made no move to expound on the past six years, Ida started pulling groceries out of the basket and lining the items on the counter. "I guess you didn't have much time for anything else but that highfalutin job your ma told me about."

Savanna could tell the statement was a compliment and took it as such. "Owning my own business does keep me busy," she said. "I spend a lot of time flying up and down the east coast, but I'm based in Baltimore."

"Your ma said your job had something to do with raising money."

Ida's statement seemed more like a question, but Savanna didn't mind. She liked nothing more than talking about her work. After all, it was the main focus in her life.

"After college-'

"Your ma preened like a peacock with that news," Miz Ida put in. "She went on and on about how proud she was that you worked your way through college with help from no one. And everybody with ears to hear had to listen to your daddy tell them how you finished a four-year degree in three."

A lump rose in Savanna's throat at the thought of her mother and daddy boasting about her. She loved her parents dearly and was happy to know they were proud of her.

They'd been hurt when she'd fled town. It had taken Savanna and her parents months to finally reconcile, and even longer to find some middle ground on which to build their new adult relationship.

But even after six years there were certain topics of conversation that were strictly off-limits, Danny Walsh, his parents, Fulton, anything that had to do with "the big scandal" were among the subjects that were never mentioned. It was best that way. Easier for everyone concerned.

Suddenly her chin dipped nearly to her chest as she realized how useless it was to lie to herself. She knew her parents followed the unwritten rule of silence, not because they wanted to or were comfortable with it, but because it was what was easiest for *her*, their only child.

Savanna noticed the silence the same time she became aware of Ida's intent gaze. Heat flushed her face, but she ignored the embarrassment at having become lost in her thoughts, and she started her story again. "After college, I landed a job for myself raising funds for a senatorial campaign. I enjoyed myself so much, I decided to give it a try professionally." She lifted her hands, palms up. "With the senator's recommendation, things just took off. And here I am with a successful career."

Ida looked at her a moment, then her forehead creased. "Well, if things are going so well for you in Baltimore, why come back to Fulton? Why buy your parents' house? Why come to such a small town, when you obviously need to be near cities and airports and such?"

Ida's frank questions weren't new. They'd been asked by the few friends she'd made in Baltimore and by her worried clients far and wide. She'd given them all the same pat answer she now offered Miz Ida. "Well, the economy is so slow right now. The house had been on the market for weeks, and Mom and Dad really wanted to move to Georgia."

Ida snorted indelicately. "It can take months to sell a house. Your parents knew that before they put out the for sale sign."

"Well," she hesitated. "I could afford to buy the house and... I wanted to do something nice for my parents." Her chin set with determination as she remarked, "It *is* a good investment. Too good for me to pass up."

"Good investment, my foot," Ida declared. "You'll be a good two-hour drive from your so-called 'good investment.' What if the roof springs a leak, or termites eat into the foundation? What if a bad storm blows through? Those things can wreak havoc. Why, there's dozens of problems that could crop up. What if the tenants don't pay the rent?

You going to keep running down here to straighten things out?"

"I hadn't really thought about it." The sentence came out sounding drawn out and lame even to her own ears.

Savanna knew exactly why she'd bought her childhood home. Even though she hadn't been back to Fulton for years, she'd always felt that, with her parents living here, she still had some small thread binding her to the town. That thread had been in danger of being cut when her mother and father announced their intentions of moving to Georgia where her father had been born and raised.

She'd fretted for weeks while the house was on the market. How could she finally make things right with everyone in Fulton if her best excuse for returning, her parents, were no longer there? She was devastated and riddled with guilt to think that she'd waited too long to right all her wrongs.

Then the answer had dawned on her; she should solve this problem as she'd learned to solve all her problems. Head-on. She needed no manufactured excuse to return to Fulton, to make things right with her friends. The fact that she could afford to buy the house and help her parents realize their dream was simply icing on the cake.

So, she wondered, if her intention was to face her demons, why was she hemming and hawing with Miz Ida's questions?

Savanna leveled her gaze at the woman and said, "The truth is, I have other reasons for coming home."

Ida simply pressed her lips together as if she were a mind reader.

"But buying the house *is* a good investment," Savanna stressed.

Miz Ida nodded. "I'm sure it is," she murmured without pausing her tally. "And it was darn nice of you to do it too."

When the final total showed in the small window of the register, Miz Ida asked, "You want these things in a box or is a bag okay?"

"A bag is fine," Savanna said, relieved that Ida didn't press her to explain her 'other reasons' for returning to town.

Ida bagged the groceries in a brown paper bag. "A salesman came in here not too long ago and tried to tell me how much money I'd save by using plastic bags instead of paper." She snickered. "He hightailed it out of here right quick when I gave him a long lecture on the environmental soundness of paper versus plastic." Making a disgusted noise, she said, "Some people think that stupidity comes with wrinkles."

"But then some people just don't think," Savanna added, chuckling.

"You can say that again." Ida looked directly into Savanna's eyes and asked, "Have you seen Daniel Walsh?"

The unexpected inquiry left Savanna momentarily speechless as she was stabbed with knife-sharp guilt. Daniel Walsh, Danny's father, had always treated her as if she were his daughter. His wife, Susan, had done the same. And Savanna, in turn, had loved them as if they were her own parents. She knew she should have talked to them, called them, *something*. But when she had first left Fulton, she hadn't been able to bring herself to contact anyone...other than the one letter she'd written to Danny, the letter he'd never bothered to answer. As the months had turned into years, Savanna had found it harder to generate the courage to get in touch. So she simply hadn't, and she'd lived for the past six years with the guilt of knowing her behavior had been inexcusable.

But she was here to fix all that. She had every intention of visiting Daniel and Susan Walsh, every intention of apologizing for her actions of six years ago.

Her thoughts of Daniel and Susan Walsh prompted a sudden, uninvited picture of their son. A crystal-clear image of the smile that gently curved Danny's mouth, of his dark eyes gazing at her lovingly just before she'd run away from him, their wedding, and the future they had spent so much time planning and dreaming about.

She clamped down on the vision, shutting it from her mind.

"No, I haven't seen him." Her tone was meek. "I just now drove into town. But I plan to." In an effort to discourage any more probing questions, Savanna asked, "How much do I owe you, Miz Ida?"

Savanna handed a few bills across the counter and received change. As she hefted the bag on her hip, she tried to smile. "I'm sure I'll see you again soon."

"You come in anytime," Ida told her. "Don't wait till you need something. Just come for a visit."

"I will," Savanna promised.

"Oh, wait." Ida scooped her hand into the large candy bowl on the counter. "Take some of these with you. They always were your favorite." Her lips drew into a grin. "You thought I forgot, didn't you?"

Savanna popped a cinnamon jawbreaker into her mouth and smiled. She waved a goodbye over her shoulder and walked out into the sunshine.

If everyone she encountered was as blunt with questions as Ida had been, Savanna mused, this visit to her hometown was going to be filled with some complicated emotions. But then she'd expected that, hadn't she? There were wrongs to right, hurt feelings to assuage. She definitely had a huge job in front of her.

* * *

Turning onto Peach Tree Drive, Savanna let the memories wash over her. As a child, she'd ridden her bike on these sidewalks, first a tricycle, then a two-wheeler. She remembered the warm, carefree breezes that would tangle her hair and turn her cheeks a bright pink as she pedaled faster and faster around the block.

Savanna sighed contentedly. *Home at last.*

The thought made her sit up straight, and a frown bit deeply into her brow. What on earth had brought that idea into her head? She wasn't planning to stay in Fulton. To the contrary, she had definite plans of returning to Baltimore and the neat little studio apartment she kept there.

As Savanna turned south onto Sycamore Lane, she marveled at the trees lining the wide street that were its namesake. Their huge, gnarled branches shrouded the asphalt with deep shadows, allowing not one shaft of sunlight to touch the pavement. She remembered these trees as being mature, she'd even climbed in them on occasion as a child. But as she ambled past them now, they didn't seem as big as the ones in her memories.

Then she saw the house. She pulled into the driveway and sat there staring, opening the floodgates of her emotions and letting them fill her to the brim.

The three-story, white Victorian home was by no means small, but the house in her memory had been a mansion, a fairy-tale castle where she had celebrated birthdays and Christmases, and had an incalculable number of sleep overs with hordes of giggling, squealing friends. This house was an unmistakable symbol of warmth, love, security.

Pressing her fingertips to her lips, she inhaled slowly, deeply, and gave herself over to the tingling sensation of happy recollection that raised gooseflesh on her arms.

She opened the car door and stepped out, surprised to discover her legs were unsteady. Clenching her fist, Savanna pressed it firmly against her stomach, trying to calm the joy, excitement, anxiety, anticipation and a thousand other feelings that churned there.

"Home." The single word passed her lips in a breathy whisper. Tears prickled behind her eyelids, and her throat seemed to swell. Her exhalation of breath was ragged with tender sentiment.

Buying this house had been the right thing to do; she knew it as surely as she knew her own name. She sniffed and fumbled in her purse for a tissue. This place meant too much to her to see it sold to strangers.

After swiping under her eyes, she let her gaze wander. The gingerbread trim that supported the eaves, the hinged shutters that flanked the long, paned windows. the white door with its beveled glass inset.

She saw other things as well; worn roof shingles, peeling paint on the wide front porch, overgrown shrubs, weed-infested flower beds that ran along the curving brick walkway. The house had been sitting empty since Savanna's mother and father had moved south more than six weeks ago. That last big campaign in Baltimore had kept Savanna from visiting Fulton before now. Her schedule was free and clear for at least the next four weeks.

"One month," she murmured. From the looks of it, Savanna felt sure she would need every day if she was going to get the house in order.

She grinned and rubbed her palms together, eager to start working. Her first act as a new homeowner was to pull up the real estate agent's sign that declared the house "SOLD" in big, bold letters. She leaned it against the cement foundation and went up the porch steps. But she reached the front door and stopped abruptly, the smile fading from her lips.

As she let her eyes rove over the thick, wooden railing, the rattan rocking chair and the porch swing, she was overcome by nostalgia, alluring memories carrying heady, sensuous overtones. This had been the very place where she and Danny had shared so many goodbyes and good-night kisses. Savanna closed her eyes. She could almost feel Danny's fingers, soft and warm, against her cheek, could almost taste his lips on hers, could almost smell the scent of his skin, could almost see the desire in his gaze.

Her eyes opened wide and she shoved the vivid memory from her.

"You know better than that," she scolded herself aloud.

Thoughts of Danny had nearly driven her mad when she'd first left Fulton. The deep, inconsolable loneliness she'd felt without him had driven her to crying jags lasting hours. For sanity's sake, she'd learned to keep busy, to close him out of her mind as quickly as possible whenever he entered her thoughts. The desolation of being without him still swept through her now and then, but, thank God, those times were rare. Being here, though, a place where they had been so close, shared so much, it was difficult to put him out of her mind. But she would.

Savanna unlocked the front door and let it swing open. Passing over the threshold was like stepping into yesterday. The smell was what was most familiar. An indefinable aroma wafted around her, a scent that, even coated with weeks of dust, could invoke only one thought. Home.

She flipped on the hall light switch and was relieved to see the glass fixture burn brightly. Flicking off the switch, she picked up the phone receiver and listened to the dial tone. She'd been in touch with the electric company and the telephone company last week to let them know when she was arriving. Her mother had left a house key with the next-door neighbor so the servicemen could get inside. Savanna made a mental note to go over and thank the woman for watching the house.

Humming a happy tune, Savanna began pulling the sheets off the furniture, listing in her mind the multitude of chores that needed doing. The list grew long in a very short time, but she wasn't dismayed. She relished the thought of making this old house all it could be again.

Savanna unpacked her things in her old room. Her mother had redecorated it in muted shades of mauve and blue. The effect was soft and tranquil.

She changed into cutoff jeans and a cotton shirt, sturdy clothes that could stand the dirt of a heavy-duty cleaning spree. Rolling up the length of her thick blond hair, she pinned it securely on top of her head.

Tramping down the stairway, she was on her way to search out a bucket and some cleaning supplies when the telephone rang.

"Hello, Langford residence." The habitual greeting slipped from her lips without a second thought.

"Savanna?" The woman's voice was shrill in her ear.

"Yes," she answered, pulling the receiver back an inch. "This is Savanna."

"I don't know if you remember me, my name is Edith Hutchinson."

"Of course, Mrs. Hutchinson. How are you?"

The woman made a clicking sound with her tongue. "Oh, you know how old age is, one ache and pain after another. But I can't complain. I am still breathing." The woman chuckled. "The reason I'm calling is that I'm with the civic welcoming committee. I was planning to see you this afternoon, but my grandson dropped in unexpectedly. He comes so rarely, I'd like to go ahead and visit with him."

"Oh, that's not a problem. I understand," Savanna assured her. "We can get together some other time."

"I'm so happy you're back in town and I'd love to come see you one day soon. But the committee really prefers that new residents meet one of us as soon as possible."

Savanna grinned. "But I'm not really a new resident."

But Edith barreled ahead as if she hadn't spoken. "I've asked Daniel Walsh to stop in this afternoon." There was a slight pause. "Do you mind, dear?"

Savanna stood speechless for a moment. It looked as though she'd be coming face-to-face with one of her main reasons for returning to Fulton sooner than she'd imagined.

"I...I don't mind at all," she stammered, her mind whirling with a dozen thoughts at once.

So Danny's father was still welcoming people to Fulton. Savanna remembered years ago her own mother had been part of the committee. Daniel Walsh had been an active member back then, spending many a Saturday carrying cakes or fresh fruit to new neighbors.

"I'd love a visit," Savanna said, this time with more certainty. Then she hesitated. "Of course I'm a mess. When was he planning to..."

"Oh, he won't mind." Mrs. Hutchinson brushed off her concern. "I'm sure he'll only stay a short while. Long enough to say hello, and welcome you back. I just called him, so he should be by any moment. He'll stop at my house first to pick up the chocolate cake I baked for you."

"Why, thank you, Mrs. Hutchinson. I'll put on the teakettle, so we can enjoy a piece of cake and a nice chat."

A tingle of anxiety swept through Savanna at the thought of facing Danny's father. Nevertheless, she was resolved to talk to the man. Granted, she hadn't expected to see him so soon, but she'd get over that. Making him understand what happened six years ago was what was important.

After saying her goodbyes to Mrs. Hutchinson, Savanna went directly to the kitchen and searched the cupboards for a kettle. Her mother had left almost everything behind, not only furniture, but dishes and pots and pans, as well. The small retirement complex where her parents had moved required only a bare minimum of essentials, and Mrs. Langford had remarked that, after thirty-two years of marriage, she deserved new appliances, furniture and anything else she wanted. Savanna had been relieved that she wouldn't have the headache of restocking the house for her prospective tenants.

She found the old whistling kettle and turned on the faucet to give it a good rinse. Nothing happened. Not one drop of water fell from the spigot.

Reaching under the sink, she turned the valve. Still no water.

"Dad must have turned off the main line," she muttered.

The door leading to the basement creaked when she pulled it open. She flipped on the switch at the head of the stairs and went down. The bare bulb threw dim light into the damp recesses. She located the main valve next to the water heater. The nozzle was tight, but finally gave way and she opened it wide. The pipes offered a loud groan as water rushed through them.

"All right," she congratulated herself, smiling.

But she hadn't taken one step toward the stairs before her attention was caught by the sound of a loud, continuous drip.

The plumbing under the large tub sink was dry as a bone, so Savanna continued her search for the leaky pipe along the walls of the basement. She was at the far side of the room, her head bent to the side as she inspected the copper lines, when a fat drop of water smacked her square on the temple.

Above her head, a steady drip was coming from a connection that had been fastened with a nut-like fixture.

"You can handle this," she told herself.

Having no idea what tools her father had left behind, Savanna found a red metal toolbox and smiled broadly when her fingers closed on a large crescent wrench that she thought would do the trick.

She'd worked hard the past six years to become self-sufficient. She wouldn't let a simple drippy pipe intimidate her. A plumber would be a complete waste of money when it was clear that all that was necessary was to tighten the connection.

Clamping the wrench on the nut, Savanna applied a little pressure, but the fitting didn't budge. She tugged harder, but the water continued to drip.

With determination in her stance, she pulled, putting every bit of her hundred and ten pounds into the action.

She shouted in triumph when the nut turned a fraction.

The tiny stream of water that ran along her arm and down her sleeve told her she'd obviously turned the nut in the wrong direction. Instantly changing the position of the wrench, Savanna pushed. Water trickled along her upraised arms, tickling her armpits and spreading a dark stain across her chest. Every muscle strained and she grunted in her effort, and again she whooped when the nut began to move.

Water burst from the pipe, striking her full in the face with force enough to cause her to drop the wrench and shield herself. The wrench whacked the top of her foot, and the resulting stab of pain made her suck in a breath. She lifted her foot and made to grab it only to be rewarded with another smack in the jaw with the spray of cold water.

Turn it off! her mind screamed. She moved in that direction and promptly tripped on the wrench, slipped on the wet floor and went down onto her hands and knees. She couldn't prevent the whispered curse that escaped from her lips.

If the main water valve wasn't shut off, the basement would become flooded. She should have thought of that before taking a wrench to the plumbing. How could she have been so stupid?

As she pushed herself up from the concrete floor, she realized the water was no longer shooting from the pipe. She swiped the rivulets of water from her eyes and cheeks. The silence of the basement was broken only by the dozens of drips coming from the overhead rafters, the copper piping, the shelving units and everything else that had been drenched by the torrent of water. Even she was dripping—from her elbows, her earlobes, her chin.

"What on earth...?" She murmured the question, bewildered as to how the water had stopped.

A sound came from the far side of the basement, shoes scuffing on concrete. She stopped breathing in order to listen, and again she heard the noise.

Every muscle tensed. She bent and snatched up

the wrench that was lying at her feet. Clutching it tightly, she called, "Who's there?"

The shadowy figure straightened and then stepped from behind the water heater, the light from the bare bulb illuminating his face. Savanna blinked, once, twice, unable to believe her eyes.

"Danny," she whispered.

CHAPTER TWO

———————

"I didn't mean to frighten you."

His voice was as rich as aged brandy and Savanna found hearing it just as intoxicating.

Say something, Savanna, her mind instructed. *Say anything.* But it was as though her brain waves couldn't connect with the facial muscles that made her mouth function.

"I knocked, but didn't get an answer," he said.

Savanna barely heard him, so intent was she on feasting her eyes on the sight of him. He'd changed in the six years she'd been gone. Age had altered him in small, subtle ways.

Laugh lines had always parenthesized his

mouth, but they were etched deeper than she remembered. The planes and angles of his face had become more defined, more rugged. His dark hair was tinged at the temples with a few strands of premature gray. That familiar strong jaw that she'd kissed so often in her youth looked even stronger, even more kissable.

Her breath caught in her throat at the thought.

"When I heard you scream," he said, "I let myself in. I followed the sounds down here. You looked as though you could use some help." He pointed toward the dark corner from which he'd emerged "So I turned off the water."

"Thanks," she murmured. Warring emotions overwhelmed her. He looked so good.

I need time, she thought. *Time to think.*

His mahogany eyes seemed to pierce right through her, and slowly, as though awaking from a deep sleep, Savanna became aware of her body's reaction to this man whom she'd left behind so many years ago.

Her heart was hammering in her chest so hard that she could feel it pounding against her rib cage. Blood surged through her body at a dizzying speed. Her chest rose and fell at an abnormal rate, and she felt the need to suck great quantities of air into her lungs. Her throat constricted and her knees felt wobbly.

"Danny, I..." Her voice trailed. This wasn't anything remotely close to the reunion she'd imagined she would have with him.

She watched his eyes close; she watched his jaw clench; she watched his nostrils flare as he inhaled quickly. She knew the action, remembered it as though it were only yesterday. He was upset.

When he finally looked at her, his gaze was cold and empty. His expression revealed an icy restraint that she'd never witnessed in him in all the years they'd been together. She searched her memory for some clue to what he might be thinking, but found none. What she did discover was the stark realization that this man was a stranger.

"You're wet to the skin," he finally said. "And it's damp down here. You should get into some dry clothes."

The advice was given in a cool, detached tone that was so different, so alien, from the Danny she used to know. There seemed to be a wall between them. A wall that was invisible, intangible, yet nonetheless solid.

She nodded numbly and moved toward him and the stairway he blocked. He stepped back to let her pass, but when she was within reach of him, she stopped. Some unseen force compelled her to look up into his face. Her throat was tight with the emotion that continued to explode inside her.

"It's so good to see you." The statement flowed from her like clear water gushing from a spring. Honest, candid, without thought.

She was surprised by what her words did to his features. A wrinkle formed between his brows as they drew together in what she took to be annoyance. His gaze darkened, erasing the cool reserve that had been there just a heartbeat before. His tight, white lips confirmed the fact that he was clearly displeased. She could see him fighting to control it.

"Go get changed," he ordered.

Her head dipped away from him and she hurried up the steps, confusion fogging all thought. The whole scene was like a bad dream. But that was wishful thinking. Having a nightmare would have been preferable to this. She couldn't make this situation go away by waking.

Moving into the hallway off the kitchen, she

raced up the steps leading to the second-floor bedrooms. She snatched a towel from the linen closet and went into her room, closing the door behind her.

She dug through the dresser drawer, snatching out dry underclothes, a shirt and a pair of shorts. Stripping off her wet things, she fought the urge to ponder on the change in Danny Walsh. But the odds were against her.

She may not have spent more than two minutes with him, but she was certain of the change. He wasn't the man she remembered. He wasn't the man she'd come so close to marrying six years ago.

That Danny had been open, friendly, caring. Someone who was quick to smile. This man seemed cold and hard... and full of anger.

But then what had she expected? She'd left Danny to face their family and friends on what should have been the most important day of his life. Of course he'd feel angry with her. What else could she expect?

"Okay," she muttered, knowing the thing to do now was to face the situation at hand. "Danny's downstairs. He's upset and angry." *Deal with it*, she told herself.

After tucking the tails of her blouse into her shorts, she slipped into a pair of strappy sandals. She went into the bathroom, drying her hair with the towel as she went. After running a brush through it, she quickly braided her hair into a single, fat rope and secured the end with a bright yellow ribbon that matched her blouse.

As she descended the stairs, her muscles balked with every step. She wanted desperately to hug him, talk to him, ask him a million and one questions about his life, but she also wanted to run out the front door, hop into her car and drive away from him and the cold glare he'd leveled on her a few minutes ago. She had to face him; she knew it as surely as she knew her own name. She only wished she had more time to think about what to say. She wasn't eager to experience his hostility, or his cool reserve. Then she had to admit that she also wasn't eager to endure the overwhelming sensations that rocked her body when she was near him. Those very physical reactions had taken her completely by surprise.

Wait a minute! She halted on the staircase. How did she know it was Danny who had caused her blood to pound and her heart to race? She'd felt a rush of adrenaline when the pipe had burst. She'd been wet. The cellar had been damp and chilly. Maybe her body's responses had been quite natural, given the circumstances.

She continued down the steps and almost had herself convinced when she rounded the corner into the kitchen and collided with Danny as he came through the doorway. She heard his sharp intake of breath. Her own surprised inhalation filled her lungs with his cologne, a dark and sensual scent, and an immediate warmth began to build in her chest.

"I'm sorry," she whispered. Raising her hands to brace herself, she grasped his hard biceps, but couldn't seem to steady her shaky knees. Her legs felt as pliable as warm clay. And the feel of his taut, knotted muscles made the warmth inside her grow hot and prickly.

His arms went around her protectively, keeping her from collapsing, and she felt her blood course through her veins like a runaway roller coaster. The wild rhythm of her heart proved in no uncertain terms that it was, and had been, Danny who caused her body's wild response.

She planted one hand firmly against his chest

with the intention of pushing away from him, but as soon as she'd made contact, the pounding of his heartbeat made her eyes fly to his. She saw a flash of something in his gaze. Panic or passion, she couldn't tell which. But as quickly as it had come, it was gone.

The next instant his expression became shuttered, unreadable. But Savanna knew that he'd been as rocked by their contact as she. Well, she thought with a flash of stubbornness, if you can deny your reaction, Danny Walsh, then so can I.

"I'm okay," she murmured breathlessly. "Really." She stepped out of his embrace and grabbed hold of a spindle-back kitchen chair as nonchalantly as possible in an effort to brace her rubbery legs. She tried to smile, but the look in his eyes told her it was a wasted effort.

Then he inhaled deeply and rubbed his hand across the back of his neck. He seemed to visibly relax now that there was some distance between them. The tightness around his mouth softened; one corner even lifted a fraction. His dark eyes cleared a bit as he said, "I mopped up some of the mess. The floor's still pretty wet, though."

"You didn't have to do that," she said.

He stared at her for another silent moment.

"You look good, Savanna." He said the words as though he'd tried his damnedest not to and had finally relented.

Pure nervous tension forced her to laugh at his strained tone. "I guess I'll take that as a compliment."

He offered a small smile, and like the sun chasing away the grayness of a cloudy day, the uneasiness that had been between them since he'd arrived vanished without a trace.

"That's how I meant it." His deep voice was soft with meaning now and conjured up all the old feelings of happiness and security that she remembered.

"You've changed," he commented. Reaching out, he took the tips of her fingers in his own and rubbed the pad of his thumb across her long, manicured nails. "You've broken some old habits, I see."

She nodded. "That one was the hardest to break."

Gazing down at her fingers in his, she went on, "It's hard to command professional respect with your fingers in your mouth. Nail biting isn't a very ladylike habit."

"I suppose not," he said. "But there's nothing about you now that isn't ladylike."

His eyes traveled down the length of her as he spoke and Savanna felt her face flame. She tightened her grip on the chair. If she let go now she was afraid she just might sink to the floor.

When his gaze lifted to hers, he asked, "How have you been?"

"Fine," she answered, her voice dry and grating. "And yourself?"

"I've survived."

"Did you marry?" As soon as the question passed her lips she felt the urge to bite off her tongue. She was mortified. What had compelled her to delve so intimately into his personal life? *Because you're dying to know*, came the simple answer.

"No."

His curt response offered no explanation and she didn't have the guts to pursue the subject further.

"I was expecting your father," she said in a rush. The shadow that crossed his face at the mention of Daniel didn't register, so intent was she to get away from the topic of marriage. She didn't want to have to admit to Danny the lonely state of her own personal life.

"When Mrs. Hutchinson called to say that Daniel was coming to welcome me back to Fulton," she continued, "I was so pleased that I'd get the chance to catch up on all the news of your family. I haven't heard a thing in all these years and I couldn't wait to talk to him."

"The folks in town call me Daniel now." His harsh tone stopped her monologue like a speeding car slamming into a brick wall.

Emotions flashed across his face so quickly that Savanna couldn't read them fast enough. Pain, sadness, irritation, until at last his features were once again so controlled she couldn't discern what he was feeling.

"They do?" Her voice was faint as she asked the question because, once again, she couldn't fathom what she'd said to prompt that look back to his face.

He shifted his weight and plunged one hand deep into his trouser pocket as he nodded. "From the first day I took over Dad's practice, everyone in town insisted on calling me Daniel."

"So Mrs. Hutchinson was talking about you," Savanna said. In that instant she remembered Miz Ida had also said Daniel. Savanna suspected the lovable old snoop had been asking if Savanna had seen Danny, not his father.

"Daniel." She tried out the name. "I don't know that I'll remember, but I promise to give it my best shot."

Her mind quickly assembled the information he'd given her and she asked, "You're here for the Fulton Welcoming Committee?"

He nodded solemnly. "I guess you could say I've taken over for my father in more ways than one."

"Your dad's retired, then?" She shook her head, smiling. "I never thought the day would come when he'd give up his law practice."

"No."

The tension in his voice as he said that single word made the smile fade from her lips. A dreadful feeling began to churn in her stomach as she stared at him, waiting for him to elaborate.

When he spoke his voice was feather soft. "You really don't know, do you?"

His question was all it took. Tears gathered in her eyes as she realized that Daniel Walsh wasn't sharing a law office with his son, that he hadn't retired to some hot, southern climate as her own parents had done. The deep sadness in Daniel's eyes told her clearly that his father had passed away and the news literally shook her.

"I'm so sorry." She wanted to say more, but her voice cracked like old glass.

Daniel pried her fingers from the chair and, pulling it out from under the table, guided her to sit down. She didn't fight him; she didn't even argue.

He knelt down in front of her and took her hands in his. His palms felt warm against her icy fingers. She tried to focus on his thumb as it slowly passed over the peaks and valleys of the knuckles of her right hand.

She needed to get control of herself so that she could tell him how much she'd loved his father.

A new thought brought a wave of fresh panic and she lifted her face to look at Danny. "Your mother?" she asked.

"She's fine," he assured her. "She's moved to Richmond to be with my sister."

Savanna exhaled audibly, relief bringing a small smile to her lips. Then she pulled one hand from his grasp to swipe at a damp wisp of her hair that was tickling her cheek. Gazing at Danny, she saw caring and concern. Every trace of hardness was gone from his eyes. Here was the man of her teenage dreams. Here was the Danny Walsh she remembered.

"I really am sorry about your father," she said. "How did it happen? And... and when?"

She felt him pull away from her, physically and emotionally. He stood and her eyes followed his movement.

"Heart attack," he informed her. "This June will be five years."

Five years! She could see by the look on his face that he was wondering how it could be that she hadn't heard the news.

"Danny." She stopped, then started again. "Daniel, there's no excuse for my not having sent your mother my condolences."

"You're right," he remarked tightly, "there's not."

"Please, let me at least try to explain," she implored. "When I first left Fulton my relationship with my parents fell completely apart. At first I was scared to death to call them. Then, when I did call, Mom refused to speak to me. It took us months to form some semblance of what could be called a relationship." Savanna stopped and swallowed hard at the painful memories of that terrible time. "It may sound hard to believe, but we never discussed what happened." She hesitated before clarifying, "My running away, I mean. To this day, we never talk about Fulton. Or your parents. Or you." She moistened her dry lips. "It's just easier for us this way. I'm sorry I didn't know about your father."

As he listened to her excuse his dark eyes began to freeze and now they looked like cold chips of onyx glittering with bitterness.

"You never thought to ask?"

His question was like a splash of freezing water. Her eyes widened and she sat up straight. He only frowned at her, waiting for an answer.

"I just told you..." Her urge to explain was engulfed in a flame of anger. "Danny, I loved your parents! I loved them just as much as I love my own."

"But not enough to ask how they were getting

on. Not enough to let them know how you were. Or where you were." Every muscle in his body was tense. "You didn't love them enough, did you, Savanna? In the end you only loved yourself."

She sat there silent, staring up at his taut face. Swallowing around the tightness in her throat, she said, "I understand your anger."

He looked away. He raised a hand and rubbed it back and forth across his jaw. When he looked at her again, his emotions were firmly under control.

"I'm not angry with you, Savanna," he said. After sighing, loud and heavy, he continued, "I guess I shouldn't have come." He raked his fingers through his hair. "Oh, hell, I meant for this to be so different. I just wanted to...I wanted..." His voice trailed off in obvious frustration.

Savanna stood. "What did you want?" Her query was soft as a whisper.

He stepped back. Whether it was involuntary or a conscious act, she couldn't tell.

His quick smile didn't quite reach his eyes as he shrugged. "To see how you were, of course. That's all."

At that moment making things friendly and comfortable again seemed all important for some reason. Savanna crossed the space between them and placed her hand on his forearm.

"Please sit down," she said. "We'll have a cup of tea or something and catch up. A lot of years have gone by."

He took another step back and her hand fell to her side. "I really can't," he said, looking at his wristwatch. "I've stayed too long as it is. I'm due at the office."

"I see."

He flashed her another of those half smiles. "I haven't done a very good job of it, but welcome to Fulton. I'm sure I'll see you around town." He turned and pushed his way out the back door.

Savanna raised her hand and called goodbye, but she was sure he hadn't heard. She looked down and saw Mrs. Hutchinson's chocolate cake on the kitchen table. Marring the smooth icing, she swiped her finger along the side of the cake. As the fudge frosting melted in her mouth, she shook her head, certain now that straightening out the mess she'd made six years ago was going to be more difficult than she'd first imagined.

* * *

Six weeks of total neglect had allowed the weeds

to take over of the flower beds. Savanna found a pair of garden gloves and started pulling. The episode with Danny...no, he went by Daniel now, she'd have to remember. The incident had left her emotionally drained and she found the mundane task of weeding somewhat restful.

"Hey, there, neighbor."

Savanna twisted around and saw a woman standing on the other side of the hedgerow.

"Hi," Savanna called. She stood and brushed the dirt from the knees of her jeans. As she moved closer, she recognized her high school classmate.

"Sheila?" she asked, incredulous. "Sheila Miller?"

Sheila grinned. "It's Thompson now."

Savanna laughed delightedly. "You married Jim! I knew you two were made for each other. I just didn't think he'd ever get up the nerve to ask you out."

Chuckling, Sheila admitted, "He didn't. I finally had to ask him."

"You're kidding?"

"Nope. Why don't you take a break and come in for a glass of juice?"

"I'd love something cold," Savanna said. She

tugged off her gardening gloves as she rounded the hedge.

"Jimmy, you come down out of that tree before you break your neck!" Sheila looked up and called out to the youngster hanging from the branch, "I want you to find your sister. I haven't seen her in the past few minutes and that always spells trouble."

Freckle-faced Jimmy dropped down from the oak tree and made a rude noise that startled Savanna.

"Jimmy," his mother threatened.

"I'm going," he relented and stalked off toward the backyard.

"Come on in," Sheila said, rubbing a hand over her pregnant belly.

"Congratulations," Savanna said, glancing down at her friend's stomach. "This will be your third?"

Sheila nodded. Once they were inside the kitchen, she turned to open the cabinet for glasses. "You just met Jimmy, the monkey in the tree. He's five. Amanda's three and she's a terror. I have to keep my eye on that child every minute."

She caught sight of her children playing in the

backyard; then she filled the glasses with juice from the refrigerator and handed one of them to Savanna. "It's so good to see you," she said, strategically positioning herself so she could enjoy a chat and keep an eye on her kids. "Tell me how you've been."

Savanna filled Sheila in on her comings and goings of the past six years. When she finished, Savanna noticed that her friend's face had an almost wistful expression.

"You know," Sheila said, "I've made marriage and family my life's work. But I do have to admit..." her voice became soft, "...there are times when I wish that I'd had the courage to run off and seek my fortune like you did."

"Oh, Sheila, don't say that."

"I mean it," she insisted. "Look at you, Savanna. You have a career. You're independent. You go where you please, when you please. No diapers, no spilled milk, no sticky fingerprints. Probably not a single mismatched sock." She sighed as though that thought alone was heaven. "But you were always different. You had something. You took a chance at grabbing that golden star," Sheila went on. "You reached, and it paid off."

"But, Sheila," Savanna said, "look around you. You have a husband, a family, a home. All the things that are important in life." The polite statement was meant as encouragement, but Savanna was surprised that the words struck such an emotional chord in her.

Sheila grinned. "Someday soon, when I'm climbing the walls and ready to tear my hair out, I just might come looking for you for some support."

"Anytime," Savanna said.

"I really meant it, though, when I said you always had something special. I don't know what it was." Sheila searched for words "An inner strength or something. Something that none of the rest of us had."

"Stop, please." She fanned her hands in the air. "You're embarrassing me. Just because I haven't been back to town for a while doesn't mean you have to pile on the compliments." Savanna ran her fingers over the condensation that had collected on the outside of her glass. "I didn't have, and don't have anything, more than you do." Savanna thought of the children playing in the yard, the man who would arrive home in time for dinner. "In fact, I'm the one who's missing..."

"But you *do*," Sheila insisted. "You always did. Daniel saw it."

Savanna's gaze shot back to Sheila at the mention of Daniel. A short, but tense silence separated the two women.

"I'm sorry, Savanna." Sheila's eyes seemed to frantically search for signs of injury her mention of the past might have triggered before she groaned. "I wish I'd learn when to keep my mouth shut."

"It's all right," Savanna assured her. "It's okay to talk about Daniel. He's part of my past, part of who I am."

Savanna was hit by a twinge of discovery in the truthfulness of her comment. But she was kept from exploring it further by Sheila's relieved sigh.

"I'm so happy to hear you say that." Sheila smiled. "Because this is a small town and you're bound to run into him."

"Oh, I already have." Savanna swallowed a sip of apple juice. "He stopped over this morning bearing tidings of welcome and a delicious chocolate cake."

Savanna could tell by the curiosity clearly written on Sheila's face that the woman was dying to know more but was too polite to ask.

Shaking her head, Savanna told the truth. "It didn't go well."

"No?" Sheila's eyebrows perked up and she leaned forward.

Shaking her head dismally, Savanna reclined against the chair back and took a moment before explaining. "He was so...different. I mean, I guess I should have expected him to be angry. But I suppose I thought he would have gotten over the brunt of it by now."

"Have you?"

The question was formidable. And unexpected. Savanna's first instinct was to become defensive, to declare that, of course, she was completely over any feelings she had for Daniel Walsh, that she'd worked through all the guilt and regret she felt about having run away. But the whole point of this trip was to face the unfinished business she'd left behind in Fulton. The whole point was to confront the guilt and pain.

"I don't know," she finally admitted. "I can honestly say I was able to put it off for a very long time." Reluctant to elaborate further about her own feelings at the moment, Savanna reverted to her original topic. Daniel. "He seemed so angry with me. But it was more than just his anger, Sheila. When I saw him, he was so... I don't know, tightly controlled. Every time he started to show an emotion, he'd cut it off. Right to the quick." She reached for her glass, but didn't take a drink. "He complimented me on how I'd changed, yet he was hardly able to smile. We talked about his father, and he didn't show a bit of the grief I know he must feel."

Sheila grinned. "That pretty much sounds like the Daniel Walsh I've always known. Always in complete control. Rather moody. Sometimes downright crotchety." Growling, she added, "A regular old grizzly bear."

Taking a moment to absorb the statement, Savanna sat quiet. Finally she frowned and softly said, "But that isn't right. Danny was never like that."

"What do you mean?" Sheila asked, her smile fading. "Of course he was." She shrugged. "Still is."

"You've got to remember," Savanna said. "Don't you recall that graduation party my mom had for all of us? Remember how Danny..." she caught herself "...Daniel was the hit of the party? He made everyone laugh, lip syncing to the records, and then making up new lyrics to the songs."

Sheila's mouth drew into a broad smile. "I do remember. He was hysterical."

"And he built that pyramid of plastic cups five feet high..."

Sheila's humor flooded into her words as she said, "And he goaded my Jim into crowning the thing with his graduation cap. The tassel unbalanced everything." Sheila was laughing openly now. "And cups flew in every direction. Your mom was furious!"

Savanna laughed so hard her eyes watered. "It was the first time I ever saw Jim in the limelight."

"Oh, my." Sheila sighed. "I'd forgotten all about that."

After taking a drink, Savanna stared off into the corner of the room. "So what happened?" Her question was contemplative, addressed more to herself than to the woman standing across the kitchen.

"To Daniel, you mean?" Sheila shrugged. "You have to admit, he's had some rough turns in his life." Then she stammered, "I mean...I wasn't implying... I didn't mean..."

"It's okay." Savanna slid both hands up and down her thighs. "I'm all grown-up. I can take responsibility for my actions." She gave a comical grimace. "I may not want to, but I will."

"I think it was more than just your leaving," Sheila offered. "When Mr. Walsh died, the folks in town just assumed Daniel would take his father's place. He was put under a tremendous amount of pressure. Then his sister got sick and Mrs. Walsh decided to move to Richmond."

"Celia's sick?"

"Breast cancer." Sheila gave a sad nod.

"Oh, no."

"Thank the Lord, she's in full remission right now." Sheila sighed. "Or, at least, that's what I've heard. But now Daniel's dealing with this trouble at the hospital..."

"Trouble?" Savanna asked, a frown creasing her forehead.

"Oh, it's a money thing. Daniel's on the board of directors. Jim's the administrator at the hospital, and he says that it's real bad. Everyone is racking their brains over what to do." Absently, Sheila rubbed the palm of her hand over her stomach. "So you see, there are lots of reasons for the change in Daniel."

"I feel awful that life has been so hard for him," Savanna said. "Maybe if I'd have stayed..."

"Now don't go thinking like that. You can't change the past."

"I know that," Savanna said, leaning closer. "But hasn't he had any... good times? Like... I don't know... did he ever have a woman in his life?"

Sheila thought a moment. "Not that I know of. I'm friends with several of the nurses at the hospital and they're all gaga over him. But Daniel is downright obsessed with his work." She hesitated a moment and then lowered her voice conspiratorially as she added, "I believe he simply doesn't trust women."

"Mom!" Jimmy came tromping into the kitchen, the screen door slamming behind him. "Amanda won't give me the shovel. She's diggin' up worms."

Sheila's shoulders sagged and she shook her head. "My Amanda does love creepy crawlies. I'd better go out there before she digs a hole to China. Do you mind? I'll only be a minute."

"Of course not," Savanna said.

Sheila went out the back door, Jimmy close on her heels.

Savanna laced her fingers around the cool glass and took in all the implications revealed in her conversation with Sheila. She shuffled the information around, assembling it in some sort of order.

It was impossible to refute the fact that her actions of six years ago had affected Daniel. Her running away on their wedding day may not have been the sole reason for the change in his personality, but Savanna was certain that she'd pushed over the first domino of trouble in his life. All the other dominoes followed; his father's death, his sister's illness, his mother's relocation, the financial problems at the hospital. And they had simply smacked one against the other until Daniel had turned into "a regular grizzly bear" as Sheila had described him.

What bothered Savanna the most was Sheila's last statement. The revelation that, in Sheila's opinion, Daniel didn't trust women. Savanna's act of fleeing Fulton had saved her from a life of wondering what she could achieve, a life of being weak and reliant and overprotected. But, in saving herself, had she irreversibly hurt the person whom she'd loved so dearly in her youth? Had she made Daniel so angry and bitter that he'd been unable to find happiness?

The questions were daunting and weighed heavily on her shoulders. Somehow she had to make it up to him. And the first thing she needed to do was explain to him why she'd left Fulton.

She rubbed her fingertips back and forth across her forehead. The first step would be to explain fully why she had run away on the day of their wedding. When he understood, he'd place the blame where it belonged and put the incident behind him. He'd be able to go on with his life. Then he'd be able to find happiness.

But a small, dark question pierced through her good intentions. And what it asked was, will he listen?

CHAPTER THREE

The next morning, Savanna looked up from her "things to do' list and saw little Amanda standing on the back doorstep, peering through the screen.

"Hello," Savanna said, wondering if Sheila knew her errant daughter had wandered from her own backyard.

"You got any wah-wee-pops?"

Savanna smiled and opened the screen door to let the toddler inside.

"I don't have any candy," Savanna said. She smoothed her hand over the little girl's head full of strawberry ringlet curls. "How about an apple?"

"Okay." Amanda pulled out a chair and settled herself at the kitchen table.

"Does your mommy know where you are?" Savanna asked.

"My mommy knows everyfing," Amanda emphatically told her.

Savanna took an apple out of the fruit bowl on the counter and handed it to Amanda. She turned toward the telephone to call the girl's mother, but Amanda's disappointed voice stopped her.

"My mommy makes it better than this," the little girl stated.

"She does?" Savanna hid a smile.

Amanda nodded. "I want the red off."

"Oh," Savanna said. "You want me to peel it for you?"

Again Amanda nodded. "And I want it in pieces. Like Mommy makes."

Savanna couldn't stifle her grin. "Okay. Peeled and in pieces." She took the apple and opened the cutlery drawer to look for a paring knife. "Coming right up. But then we need to call your mom. I don't want her to worry."

Sheila's voice came drifting in with the late-morning breeze as she yelled her daughter's name.

Going to the back door, Savanna stepped out and called, "Sheila, she's over here." When she saw that Sheila was coming across the yard, Savanna went back inside and finished chopping up the apple.

She placed the bowl of apple in front of Amanda.

Amanda's nose wrinkled as she gazed at the coarsely cut fruit. Savanna barely held her laughter in check when the little girl announced, "Mommy's apples look better."

Finally Amanda heaved a resigned sigh, picked up a hunk of apple and took a dainty bite. She chewed a moment and looked up at Savanna.

"Mommy's apples taste better too."

"Amanda Thompson!" Sheila pulled open the screen door and stepped into the kitchen. "I heard that. You'll hurt Miss Savanna's feelings."

"It's all right," Savanna assured her.

Amanda turned wide, innocent eyes toward her mother. "But, Mommy, your apples do taste better."

"That's enough young lady," Sheila cut in, lifting her "mother finger" and shaking it at her daughter. "Did you say thank-you?"

"Fank you," came Amanda's automatic response. She reached into the bowl and helped herself to another chunk of apple.

"I was going to call to let you know she was here," Savanna told Sheila, "but Amanda had me busy taking the 'red' off."

"Children." Sheila rolled her eyes heavenward. "What can I say?"

"What I want to know is," Savanna said, "what do you do to an apple to make it taste better?"

Sheila chuckled. "Who knows? Sprinkle it with motherly love, maybe?"

Both women laughed.

"Listen," Sheila said, "I'm taking the kids to the park. The Ladies' Auxiliary is hosting a flea market to benefit the hospital. Jim's already there helping to set everything up. Want to come along?"

"I haven't been to a flea market in years. I'd love to go."

"Good!" Sheila pressed her hands together. "And after we spend our money buying some things we don't need, we'll take the kids to the playground and we'll have lunch. I'll pack a picnic basket."

"What can I bring?" Savanna asked.

"A few of those apples would be nice," Sheila said.

Amanda looked at the two women, a severe expression on her face and said, "Mommy bwing apples."

Savanna laughed openly. "I know, Mommy's apples taste better."

Sheila smoothed back Amanda's hair affectionately. "You little urchin," she said, and then she kissed her daughter on the forehead.

"The park is this way," Jimmy Thompson informed Savanna.

"Miss Savanna knows where the park is," Sheila told her son. "She grew up in Fulton."

"You did?" Jimmy asked.

"I sure did," Savanna said. She glanced back to check on Amanda who was sitting in the red wagon that Savanna was pulling behind her. "I climbed the trees, slid down the sliding boards, played on the teeter-totters..."

"The what?" Jimmy interrupted.

"You know, the seesaws."

"They had seesaws way back in the olden days?"

Sheila laughed. "Yes, son. We did. Gee, the way

you talk, you'd think Miss Savanna and I are old ladies."

"Oh, no, Mom, you're not old," he said gallantly. "Yet."

"Intelligent young man you have there," Savanna said to Sheila in a lowered voice.

The Fulton Municipal Park brought back a whirlwind of happy memories for Savanna. She'd spent many a sunny afternoon in this wooded area with her mother.

"Hi, Miz Ida," Jimmy called out.

Miz Ida patted the boy on the head. "Hi, Jimmy. How are you?"

"I'm real good."

"Sheila, Savanna," Ida greeted. Then she smiled down at Amanda. "And how's the day treating you, Miss Amanda?"

"Got any wah-wee-pops?"

Miz Ida hooted with laughter. "You are so cute." Then she fished around in her pocket. "Let me see what I have for these children," she said. She pulled out two lollypops and handed them to Sheila.

"Wah-wee-pop! Wah-wee-pop!" Amanda chanted.

"After lunch," Miz Ida said. "If you eat all your lunch, then you can have a sweet." Then Ida turned her attention to Savanna. "I thought I might see you today, so I brought something just for you."

Handing Savanna a cinnamon jawbreaker, Ida warned, "But you must eat your lunch first."

"Yes, ma'am," Savanna dutifully replied and smiled her thanks. She tucked the candy away, looked at all the tables covered with secondhand goods for sale and then gazed at Miz Ida. "This is great. Did you have a hand in organizing this?"

Ida nodded. "Me and the other Ladies of the Auxiliary felt we had to do something. I hate the thought of losing our hospital."

"Things are that bad?" Savanna was shocked.

"My Jim certainly thinks so," Sheila said quietly.

"Folks are traveling to the bigger hospitals in Richmond," Ida said. "They just don't realize the jobs they're putting in jeopardy every time they spend money at another hospital to have a test, or have surgery."

"I've heard people from Fulton complain that our little hospital doesn't have the same modern equipment as the newer hospitals in Richmond."

Sheila's face took on a thoroughly disgusted look. "Can't people figure out that if they don't spend their money here, Fulton General can't afford to buy new equipment? Or pay for more doctors? More nurses?"

"This measly little effort won't bring in much money," Miz Ida commented.

"But it'll shed a little light on the problem. At least the Ladies are doing something," Sheila complimented Ida. "As opposed to sitting on their backsides doing nothing."

Savanna scanned the tables of used clothing, books, puzzles, lamps and a thousand other household articles instantly positive that the items wouldn't convert into the kind of cash the hospital must need, not if the institution was on the verge of closing.

What Fulton General Hospital needed was a fund-raising idea that would earn a huge amount of money. A fund-raising idea that a professional such as herself might be able to organize.

"You know," she said to the two women, "I just might be able to help. I wouldn't mind giving you a few ideas. I do this kind of thing all the time."

"Why, of course you could!" Miz Ida was quick

to grasp the offer. "You come to Tuesday night's meeting at the hospital."

"Meeting?" Savanna's brows lifted in question.

Sheila nodded. "The hospital board meets every Tuesday evening. The main topic lately has been our pitiful lack of funds."

"You're on the board, Miz Ida?" Savanna asked.

"Have been for some time now," she said. Lowering her voice conspiratorially, Ida added, "Between seeing customers at the store, my doin's with the Ladies and my time spent tending to hospital affairs, I have no trouble keeping up on the whole town's comings and goings."

Savanna had to laugh. Miz Ida hadn't changed a bit.

"Speaking of the store, I need to run," Miz Ida said. "Got to keep those young fellas I hired on their toes."

"I was going to invite you to share our picnic." Sheila's disappointment was genuine.

"Thank you kindly. But I only stopped by long enough to see that there were plenty of tables. Your wonderful husband had them set up before I arrived." She chuckled to herself and leaned toward them, whispering, "I also came to make sure that Loraine wasn't in charge of the money. That woman is lovable, but—" she tapped her temple with her index finger "—the gray matter's fading, if you know what I mean."

Sheila did her best to ignore this all-too-true statement concerning the aging town librarian and asked, "By the way, where is Jim?"

"Last I saw of him," Miz Ida said, "he was over by the bake table."

Groaning, Sheila searched the crowd for her husband. "He's going to go off his diet. I should have come earlier with his lunch."

"Well, you all have a nice day. I'm off." Ida waved to the little ones before traipsing off toward the parking lot.

Sheila looked at Savanna. "Let's go find Jim," she said. She picked up the lunch basket and called to her son to follow. "Do you really think you could do something to help us keep the hospital going?" Sheila asked Savanna.

Savanna checked to see if Amanda was sitting before she tugged on the wagon. "I think so. What we need is something big, something really grand."

"Savanna." Sheila smiled fondly. "You said *we*."

Hitching one shoulder, Savanna said, "Well, I

was born in Fulton General. Had my tonsils taken out there. A doctor in the emergency room put three stitches in my chin when I fell in the school yard." Savanna pushed her bangs back from her forehead. "That hospital employs a lot of people. I'd hate to see them out of work. Fulton General did a lot for the community when I was growing up. I'm sure it still has a lot to offer. And just because I moved away, doesn't mean I don't care."

"Okay, okay." Sheila laughed. "There's no need to become defensive. I wasn't giving you a hard time. I was grateful that you included yourself with the rest of us who want to do something."

"I do want to help." Savanna's voice sounded far off to her own ears, so preoccupied was she with all the possibilities that floated in her head. If she did this job right, she could really help this small community. She'd feel terrific if she could give something back to Fulton, the town that had given her such wonderful childhood memories.

Let's see, she thought, a carnival might work. With clowns and games and kiddie rides. Or a...

"Savanna?"

Sheila's sharp jab in the ribs brought Savanna to instant attention.

"Hmm…" The sound snagged in Savanna's throat when she looked up and saw Daniel standing in front of her. She stopped short and little Amanda nearly tumbled out of the wagon.

While Sheila shushed her affronted daughter, Savanna was left pinned by Daniel's dark gaze.

"Hello, Savanna."

Why did the sound of his voice do such crazy things to her insides?

"Hi," she said.

Jim Thompson called out a greeting to his family as he joined the small group. Savanna turned and saw the man ruffling his son's hair. He nodded a shy greeting at Savanna.

"Nice to see you again, Savanna," he said. "Sheila told me you were back in town."

"It's nice to be back."

He shook Daniel's hand. "Thanks for helping with the tables."

"No problem," Daniel told him.

Jim offered his wife a gentle smile. "You brought lunch. That's good because I'm starved." He directed his gaze at Daniel. "You worked hard this morning. How about a sandwich?"

"Oh, we shouldn't do that to Sheila," Daniel protested. "She didn't plan on feeding a crowd."

"My wife," Jim butted in, "always expects the unexpected." He grinned and pulled Sheila to him. "And she always packs enough for an army. Why do you think I look like this?"

Sheila hugged Jim. "Oh, yes," she agreed, "there's always plenty of food." She turned adoring eyes on her husband and gave his paunch an affectionate pat. "But if you blame this on me..."

"Come here, you." Jim's sultry tone was for Sheila's ears only

Savanna discreetly turned her head as Jim nuzzled his wife's neck. She watched as Daniel also redirected his gaze. There seemed to be nowhere else for them to look but at each other.

Heat rose to her cheeks. She couldn't fathom why a simple, completely natural kiss between Sheila and Jim would make her so uncomfortable, but she was certain that it had something to do with the fact that she and Daniel used to engage in the same affectionately expressive behavior.

"Do you mind?"

Daniel had stepped closer to her, and his question took her completely off guard. Did she mind what? she wondered. That Jim was kissing his wife? That Daniel used to do the same to her?

Her blank expression must have explained her confusion for he added, "My having lunch with you and the Thompsons."

Her face flamed even hotter. "Of course not," she said, her voice clipped and unnatural.

"Let's go find a nice shade tree," Jim said, taking the basket from Sheila.

The men were several steps ahead of the women, and Sheila took the opportunity to quietly ask Savanna, "Do you mind if Daniel has lunch with us?"

"Of course not." Again, Savanna heard the short, sharp words come out of her mouth. "Really," she added, hoping she'd softened her tone enough to hide the anxiety that roiled in the pit of her stomach.

What was there to be nervous about? she silently chided herself. Sheila and Jim were with her. And Jimmy and Amanda would demand much of the focus. Really, there was nothing be anxious about. So why did she feel like a teenager with a bad case of first-date jitters?

* * *

They walked across an open field to the picnic area, and Daniel took the children to the playground while Sheila, Jim and Savanna set out lunch. They spread the blanket on the grass beneath the leafy branches of a stately oak tree.

Savanna straightened one corner of the blanket and her gaze was pulled to where Daniel played with Sheila's children. He swung Amanda high in the air and she squealed with glee. Then he chased Jimmy around the sliding board. And when it was Jimmy's turn to chase, Daniel slowed his pace until the little boy caught him.

"Lunch!" Sheila called.

Daniel lifted Amanda into his arms for one last flight into the air before he herded both children across the grassy expanse toward the picnic area. A tender smile curled the corners of Savanna's mouth when she saw him chase one wandering child, then the other.

"He's very good with the kids," Savanna remarked to Sheila.

"He is," Sheila said. Her smile quickly turned to a frown as Jimmy ran up behind his sister and pushed her hard.

Amanda tumbled off her feet and her sharp cry

sent all the adults rushing to help. Daniel picked her up, and by the time Jim, Sheila and Savanna reached them, he'd brushed the grass from Amanda's hands and knees.

"Oh, baby," Sheila cooed as she took her daughter from Daniel. The toddler buried her face in the crook of her mother' s neck.

"James Allen Thompson!" The stern voice of Jimmy's father made the boy's bottom lip quiver. "You are in serious trouble."

"It was an accident, Dad," It was clear Jimmy didn't expect anyone to believe the blatant fib.

"That was no accident," Sheila said.

"But I didn't mean it."

"Not one more word, young man," Jim interrupted his son. "You'll spend the afternoon in your bedroom for this."

"Jim," Sheila said, "this bump on Amanda's head needs ice. We should probably go home."

"Okay," he said. "My car's in the lot. I'll carry her." The still sobbing Amanda slid from one parent to the other.

"I'll pick up the lunch things," Savanna offered, "and meet you in the parking lot."

Jim shook his head. "You and Daniel stay and

enjoy lunch. I hate to say it, but I don't have room for you in the car. The back seat is loaded boxes, and with the kids' car seats..." He left the rest of the sentence unspoken as he kissed Amanda's tear-streaked cheek. "Okay, honey," he crooned over her sobs. "We'll be home soon."

Sheila shot Savanna an apologetic look.

"It's okay," Savanna whispered to her. "I'll be fine. Go take care of Amanda."

Savanna watched the Thompsons make their way to the car, Jim cradling little Amanda, Sheila with Jimmy's hand firmly in hers.

"You never know what kids are going to do next."

Daniel's sad statement made her turn her attention to him. His dark eyes were filled with remorse, so much so that Savanna touched his arm.

"There was nothing you could have done to prevent that."

"I know," he said. "But that was a nasty bump on little Amanda's head."

"Well, Sheila will take her home and put a cold washcloth on it.' Savanna smiled. "And Jim will make over her until it's all better. That's what parents do."

"And poor Jimmy..." Daniel let the sentence lag.

"I'd hate to be in his shoes this afternoon," Savanna agreed.

Savanna realized that the tumultuous scene had drained her of every vestige of nervous energy that had built up in her chest. She looked at Daniel and found the idea of spending some quiet time with him quite pleasing. She'd wanted the chance to talk to him. Maybe, if she eased into the conversation the right way, this could be the perfect opportunity.

"How about some lunch?" she asked.

Daniel's eyes searched her face. Finally he said, "We don't have to do this, Savanna. It's all right. I'll head on home and grab something to eat there. But I will help you clean up."

He dipped his head and went to move past her where the picnic was spread out under the tree. Savanna reached out and stopped him with the barest of touches.

"Please, Danny. Have lunch with me. Let's talk."

Again his dark eyes scanned hers, deeply, probingly. She felt the corded muscles of his forearm beneath her fingertips. He masked his emotions expertly, so Savanna couldn't tell exactly what was going through his mind.

After the eternity of several seconds had passed, she felt him relax, saw his eyes lose some of their intensity. He covered her hand with his own.

"Sure," he said softly.

They walked to the blanket, her hand in the crook of his elbow, his hand gently on hers. The serene aura that surrounded them conjured misty emotions in Savanna. She didn't know why things had taken such an amiable turn, and she refused to question it. Her only thought was to spend some time with Daniel, the man who had meant so much to her so long ago.

As they feasted on Sheila's delicious Southern fried chicken and homemade rolls, they talked endlessly about how they'd spent the past six years. He told her about his sister's fight with breast cancer, a fight she, so far, was winning. He spoke of his mother and how she hadn't wanted to leave Fulton but had felt torn because Celia needed her. Daniel's voice was quiet when he talked about his father's death. The turmoil of taking over his father's law practice had been tremendous it seemed, but Daniel's tone lightened when he revealed the great amount of support the community had given him when he'd taken on the challenge.

Then it was Savanna's turn. She told him all about the lean years she spent acquiring her education. She'd refused her parents' offer of funds, not meaning to hurt them in any way, but as a means of reinforcing her commitment to demand her own maturation, independence and sense of responsibility. It was something she'd simply had to do for herself.

When she said those last few words, she saw a trace of white outlining Daniel's compressed lips, the only indication of his discomposure.

Savanna spent a silent moment wrapping up the remaining chicken and putting it in the basket. Daniel was quiet and she thought that perhaps she needed to change the subject.

Looking over at him, she could see he was content to just sit quietly. The lull in conversation was by no means uncomfortable and she considered relaxing in the tranquility of simply being here. With Daniel. Something, over the last few years, she'd grown to believe improbable if not entirely impossible. But she didn't feel all talked out yet. And besides, she needed to somehow broach the subject of his feelings about their past. Initiating some dialogue would be a start in the right direction.

She tossed him a shiny red apple and then plucked one from the basket for herself. "It sure is a beautiful day."

"Sure is," Daniel agreed, then bit into the fruit.

She tried again. "You know, I never forgot what a wonderful town Fulton is. People still care about one another here. It's not like that where I live. I hardly know my neighbors. I'd love to be able to come home to stay."

Daniel remained silent and Savanna clearly saw her attempt to start a conversation fall flat. Butterflies fluttered in her stomach as the silence grew strained.

"I..." They spoke the same word at the same time and then both stopped abruptly.

Savanna chuckled. "Please," she said, "go ahead."

Daniel shrugged. "I was just going to tell you that I'm glad you could get Harvey to fix your plumbing last night."

"But..." Savanna couldn't help the frown of confusion that marred her brow. "How did you know?"

Now it was Daniel's turn to chuckle. "Savanna, you've been in the big city too long. You're back in Fulton. A town where everybody knows everything about everyone. I found out Harvey worked on your plumbing the same way I found out you weeded your flower beds yesterday afternoon. The same way I found out..." his eyes lightened with suppressed humor "...that you spent an ungodly sum of money at the supermarket on convenience foods this morning."

"Okay, okay," she mumbled. "I get the picture. The dreaded small-town grapevine." She eyed him a moment, daring him to laugh, then said, "Well, a girl's gotta eat, doesn't she?"

He finally surrendered to the merriment that danced in his eyes, and Savanna wasn't long in joining him in laughter.

Finally Savanna inhaled deeply of the fresh air. "This park brings back such wonderful memories for me."

"I feel the same," he said quietly.

"My mom used to bring me here." Savanna

gazed over at the playground. "She'd push me on the swing until I thought I'd touch the clouds."

"Oh."

She looked at Daniel. "What?" she asked. He seemed so disappointed at the mention of her memory.

"When you said the park brings back memories," he began, "I thought you meant..." He shook his head. "Never mind."

"What?" she pressed. "I'd like to know what you thought I was talking about."

Daniel just shook his head, silently refusing to say more. But the light in his gaze and the delicious grin hovering at the corners of his mouth triggered a memory.

Her lips spread into a broad smile. "I haven't thought about that night in years." She settled back against the trunk of the oak tree. "There was a new moon. And about a zillion stars twinkled in the sky. It was so hot that night. But as you walked me home from the movies holding my hand, I wouldn't have cared if it was raining molten lava."

"I knew it was late," Daniel picked up the story. "I shouldn't have suggested we cut through the park. I shouldn't have lured you to sit on the bench, to linger under the stars, but I couldn't help myself."

"Daniel Walsh, you mean to tell me there was an ulterior motive attached to your suggestion of a shortcut through the park?"

His face actually tinged with pink, but Savanna's open laughter told him she was teasing.

"I was a red-blooded American boy, through and through," he admitted.

"That was the most romantic night of my life." Savanna curled her legs beneath her. "My first date. My first kiss. It was all so wonderful."

"Wonderful?" Daniel's frown drew his brows together. "I was sweating like a roasted pig. And we'd barely touched lips before Marty shined that damned flashlight in my eyes."

"Don't you mean..." she mocked a deep, manly tone "...you'll-call-me-Officer-Brown-and-like-it?"

"He'd graduated high school a year ahead of me. Marty earned that badge and his head swelled twice its normal size."

Laughter bubbled up from Savanna's throat. "I thought I'd die when he threatened to arrest you if you didn't take me directly home. I was so embarrassed, and so afraid you'd never call me again. I felt horrible that he gave you such a hard time."

"He wasn't the only one who gave me a hard time." Daniel grimaced. "I was scolded by every person I came into contact with for the next week. Miz Ida topped the list. When I ran into the Kwik-E Mart to buy my mother a pint of milk, Miz Ida demanded to know my intentions where you were concerned. And, I swear, Marty Brown actually growled every time I saw him."

"Stop," Savanna pleaded. "I can't laugh anymore. My stomach muscles are aching."

Daniel gazed at her with dark, serious eyes. He leaned over and brushed her hair from her cheek. "I do agree, though up until that point..." he let his thumb slide down her jawline "...it was a romantic evening."

He let his hand drop, but he remained close enough for her to smell his cologne, a dark, wild fragrance that enticed a woman to do things she might later regret.

She shook her head to clear the sensual thoughts. She and Daniel were sharing a heartfelt memory, that was all.

"We certainly did have some good times together," she remarked.

"We did."

Impulsively she reached out and touched her hand to his knee. "Oh, Danny, I'm so sorry I ran away like I did."

He drew away from her, but her verbal momentum surged ahead and she continued. "But I had to. I just *had* to, can't you see? It wasn't your fault. It was *me*. I tried to explain all that."

"*Explain?*" His voice nearly cracked as it elevated in tone. "You never tried to explain anything."

Savanna had never before seen such a lightning-fast change in a person's demeanor. One moment Daniel had been calm and serene in his reminiscence, the next he was a mass of bitter energy. His body had gone as stiff as the wood in the tree behind her. He'd actually pinched up a handful of the blanket beneath them.

"But I did," she protested. "I wrote you…"

Daniel just shook his head. "You may have meant to leave a note. You may have meant to get in touch with me, call me, something. But you never did." His eyes narrowed and he savagely repeated, "You never did."

Savanna opened her mouth to speak, but before she could get any words out she saw him struggle with the anger he felt. He took only a split second to control himself and slide a blank mask down over his features. She was awed by the fact that he could so thoroughly hide such explosive emotion.

"I think I should go."

"Daniel," she said, "we have to talk about this. It isn't right for you to deny your feelings this way."

"There's nothing to deny or confess." The words were short and sharp.

"There is," she refuted. "You are angry with me. You're angry that I ran away from our wedding. You're angry that I left you to face our friends."

"I am not."

Savanna pursued relentlessly. "You're angry that I left you to explain everything to your parents. And mine." She moved closer to him. "You're angry that I left you to face the town. All alone." She leaned even closer and she lowered her tone in an effort to gain the biggest impact as she said, "You, Daniel Walsh, are so full of outrage that you don't even know how to deal with it."

His control snapped and his ire glittered brightly in his brown eyes. Savanna felt an instant of triumph, but it was quickly quashed and replaced by uncertainty when he reached up with both hands and firmly cupped her face.

"I guess there's just one way," he whispered, "to prove you wrong." And he covered her mouth with his.

Savanna felt as though she were under siege of his lips, not as if she were being kissed by them. His attack was hot. Fierce. His eyes were wide open and so were hers.

Panic flitted around the edges of her brain, but before the emotion could fully take hold, Daniel ended the kiss by jerking away from her.

"There," he said, his voice ragged as torn cloth. "That ought to prove it once and for all."

He got to his feet and stomped off across the open field, leaving Savanna gaping.

CHAPTER FOUR

Daniel slammed the door of his office and stalked across the room. How could he have done something so damned stupid?

He swore under his breath and raked his fingers through his hair. The view from the window showed a calm Sunday afternoon that was a monumental contrast to the fury simmering in the pit of his gut. He was so angry with himself!

Nearly the whole town had been in the park this afternoon. All of them had been watching as he'd had lunch with Savanna. Everyone had seen him kiss her. Hell, he'd practically assaulted the woman.

God, what had he been thinking, kissing her like that? He'd been nothing short of forceful and domineering. His effort to prove he wasn't angry had only served to prove the exact opposite. It were as if he'd been out to kill a spider with a sledgehammer.

He rued the day Savanna Langford had returned to Fulton. Murmurings from different people had alerted him days before Savanna had actually arrived. Daniel had refused to give the situation much thought, really, remembering what his father used to say, "Don't worry until you know there's something to worry about. Don't pay interest on a loan you may never owe."

After Savanna arrived, the word around Fulton was that she wasn't planning on staying for long. Daniel had been surprised by the tremendous relief he'd experienced when he'd learned that news. It had felt as though he'd been permitted to suck in a lungful of cool, fresh air after having held his breath longer than was prudent.

Savanna was visiting Fulton for a month or so. He could live with that. Surely he could smile when he saw her, could politely ask how she was. He'd tolerate her visit, and then he'd gladly escort her to the town limits when she was ready to go back to wherever it was she had come from. He'd felt confident that he could handle the few situations that would arise when he'd be in her company.

But he hadn't. In fact, he'd failed miserably. Of the two times he'd seen her this weekend, the first he'd lost all control of his normally tightly reined emotions and had run like a frightened rabbit out the back door of her house, the second he'd once again lost control and...

"Damn!" The curse echoed off the walls.

What the hell had happened today?

He paced to his desk and sat down.

That fiasco of a kiss wouldn't have happened if Savanna Langford hadn't pushed him beyond the brink. Who did she think she was to come back into town—*his town*—and confront him about the past? The woman was obviously suffering from grand delusions to accuse him of harboring anger against her all this time. How could he be angry with someone he hadn't thought about for six years?

He scrubbed at his face with open palms.

That wasn't quite true, he had to admit. Daniel

put his elbow on his desk and rested his forehead in his hand. He'd thought about her over the years, but not because he'd wanted to.

He could remember many hot, sultry nights when the moonlight and thoughts of Savanna would draw him out into the darkness to walk the streets of Fulton. And during those times he was nearly driven mad by the crystal-clear images that formed in his head; the way the moonbeams turned her hair to liquid silver, the way she'd lift her chin and gaze at him with those huge blue eyes, the way her lips would purse softly as she waited for his kiss.

Then, unable to stop them, Daniel would suffer as his other senses would spark even more vivid memories. He could actually smell the fresh flowery fragrance of her hair, or the scent that he smelled every time he buried his face in the curve of her neck, a delicate, heated scent that drove him absolutely crazy. If he concentrated, he could literally feel the way her small hand used to fit in his, or the silkiness of her skin under his fingertips, under his lips.

He rose swiftly and stalked to the window. What was the matter with him? He could feel the pain building steadily. He'd thought he'd dealt with all of this sentimental mind-clutter concerning Savanna. He'd been certain he'd tamped it down until he'd pushed it so far in the back of his brain that he could finally forget the past. Until he could finally live with what she'd put him through. And he *had* lived with it. Until now.

"Just hang in there," he murmured. "She won't be here long."

Suddenly he paled. What had she said during lunch? He searched his short-term memory for her exact words, but he couldn't seem to recall them. She'd said something to the effect that she liked the idea of living in a small town. No, no, he thought, that wasn't it exactly. His mind ran in a frantic attempt to remember. She'd said that she'd love to move to Fulton.

His heart raced. If having Savanna in town for two short days had rattled him to this extent, how in heaven's name could he exist living in the same town with her?

Impulsively he turned sharply on his heel and pulled open the top drawer of the filing cabinet nearest the window. He flipped through the manila folders. The letters were here someplace, he'd filed them himself.

When he had his hand on the folder, he relaxed a bit and took it over to his desk. He settled himself in his chair and opened the file. The senior partner of Richmond's largest law firm had sent him a partnership proposition annually for the past three springs running. Daniel had politely turned down each offer, but he'd kept the letters.

He stared at the latest offer, but he was so agitated he couldn't seem to focus on the words. If he lived in Richmond, he'd be near his mother. If he was working in Richmond, he'd be near Celia. If he moved away from Fulton, he wouldn't have to worry about running into Savanna. He wouldn't have to run the risk of ever again losing his cool around her.

Daniel didn't know exactly what Savanna's plans were, didn't know if she was going or staying. But it wouldn't hurt for him to keep all of his options open. It wouldn't hurt a bit for him to prepare for the worst.

Without giving the matter another thought, he picked up his voice recorder and began dictating a letter of inquiry.

* * *

Savanna turned onto a winding street of a suburb of Richmond. She glanced down at the directions that Daniel's mother had given her over the phone, then she looked up and began counting the houses on the left side of the street.

Susan Walsh had been the epitome of the genteel Southern lady when Savanna had telephoned the woman barely an hour ago asking if they could get together. Savanna had tried to keep the distress out of her voice, but wasn't certain if she'd succeeded. When Daniel had denied any knowledge of having received her letter of explanation, Savanna had been confused at first. Then she began thinking that maybe his parents had kept the letter from him in an effort to protect him. Or maybe the letter had been lost in the mail.

Enough speculation, she had thought. If she wanted answers to her questions, the best place to go was directly to a knowledgeable source: Daniel's mother. With the help of the internet phone book, Savanna had easily obtained the Richmond telephone number of Daniel's sister, where his mother now lived. Susan Walsh hadn't sounded in the least surprised to hear from her. She'd only sounded pleased. Savanna wondered if Daniel had talked to his mother about her arrival in Fulton.

Savanna pulled into the long asphalt driveway of a large, white Georgian-style home. A huge magnolia tree partially blocked her view of the house. She stopped the car and cut the engine.

She hadn't planned on meeting Daniel in the park earlier today. And she hadn't expected this drive to Richmond to see Susan Walsh, either. Nothing about her visit south had turned out the way she'd planned. But then didn't some smart person once say that the best laid plans often went awry? If she wasn't feeling such turmoil, she'd probably laugh at the irony.

The soles of her shoes scuffed on the brick-paved walkway, and once she reached the front step she pressed the doorbell.

The door swung open almost immediately, and Savanna found herself in the warm embrace of Daniel's mother.

"Savanna," the woman said, pulling back at arm's length, "you look so lovely. So all grown up."

"Hello, Mrs. Walsh."

"Susan, dear. Being called Mrs. Walsh makes me feel my age." The woman chuckled and then took

Savanna's hand and tucked it in the crook of her arm, leading her inside.

"I'm sorry about your husband," Savanna said. "I just learned the news. I'm awfully sorry I didn't attend the funeral...send a card, flowers, something."

Susan waved away her concern. "Honey, you couldn't do any of those things if you didn't know, now could you?" She patted Savanna's hand. "Now, let's go into the living room and have a nice chat."

Once they were settled on the couch in a large, bright sitting room, Savanna turned slightly sideways so she would face Susan.

"First off," Savanna began, "I want to apologize and explain what happened when..."

Daniel's mother stopped her with one upraised index finger. "Now listen to me," she said gently. "I expect no explanation. And there's no apology needed. It all happened a long time ago."

"But..." Savanna stopped when Susan closed her eyes and shook her head.

Susan's dark eyes, so much like her son's, conveyed kindness and understanding when she said, "Savanna, we can't plan life's twists and turns."

Savanna's heart went out to her. What with Daniel's near miss of a wedding, her husband's death and her daughter's illness, Susan's life had certainly consisted of many unexpected twists and turns.

"All we can do," the woman went on, "is deal with them the best way we can. I've always been confident that you were only dealing with your life the best way that you knew how." Her voice lowered as she added, "My husband felt the same. He told me so many times."

Tears of gratitude burned Savanna's eyes and she whispered, "Thank you."

The two tiny words couldn't possibly express the relief that Susan's understanding gave her, but it was the only phrase she could come up with that might begin to express how she felt.

"Now," Susan said, smiling. "You seemed a little distraught on the telephone. It's important that we talk, isn't it?"

"Well...yes."

"And it's about Daniel, isn't it?"

Savanna exhaled plaintively. "As a matter of fact..."

"I knew as soon as I heard your voice on the phone." With that, Susan settled back against the couch and waited for Savanna's explanation to unfold.

Rubbing her palms on the thighs of her trousers, Savanna gazed around the beautifully decorated room, trying to shuffle her words into the right order before she spoke them. She looked at Daniel's mother and saw not a trace of impatience, and she was grateful.

"Well, I saw Daniel today," Savanna began. "I had lunch with him, in fact."

Susan's eyes lit with surprise, but she remained silent.

Finally Savanna scooted to the edge of her seat and leaned closer. "Daniel is very upset. In fact, he's angry. He is so furious with me. I can feel it. I can see it." She tucked a strand of her hair behind her ear and thought she'd better back up and start the story of her visit to Fulton from the beginning. "You see, I came home because I felt I needed to explain things to him." She splayed her hand on her chest. "For my own sake. I've felt for a very long time that I had some unfinished business that I needed to deal with. Sort of like a dangling rope that needed to be secured."

Savanna sat back, inhaled deeply and exhaled before she continued. "I thought I'd come home and see Daniel, talk to him. But when I did, I saw that he is so...so..." She looked at Susan in frustration. "Angry," she finished.

"And hurt," Susan added quietly.

"Yes." Savanna was once again on the edge of the couch cushion. "I knew when I ran away that Daniel would be hurt. I never should have left him to face everyone alone. But I was frantic. I was scared and..."

"You were so very young, Savanna," Susan said. "Stop being so hard on yourself."

Savanna felt regret and sadness well up inside of her until the emotions threatened to overflow. Tears blurred her vision and she realized that she'd somehow gotten off the beaten track. She hadn't meant to come here and bare her soul. She wanted—no, she *needed* answers to some very sticky questions.

But how could she ask this proper Southern lady if she'd waylaid the letter that Savanna had written to Daniel? How could she accuse Daniel's mother of keeping from him the one thing that would have explained her actions? If Susan Walsh had kept the letter from her son in an effort to spare him any more hurt, she may have only succeeded in prolonging Daniel's angry feelings. Prolonging them for six years.

Savanna didn't know how she could bring herself to ask, she only knew she had to know.

"Susan, while Daniel and I had lunch today," she said, "we talked a little." She smiled when she remembered the fond memory of their first date that they had shared. "The conversation eventually led to the subject of my fleeing town six years ago." She sighed. "It was inevitable, I guess, since I had planned to talk to him sometime during my visit, anyway." She folded her hands in her lap. "Anyway, I talked to him. I tried to explain that it was all my fault. But he only seemed to grow even more angry."

Savanna coughed nervously. Anxiety knotted in her throat and she found it hard to form the words she wanted to say.

"I told him that I had written to him," she said slowly.

She waited to see what response Susan would have to her statement. Savanna expected to see the woman lower her eyes guiltily or dip her head when she realized she'd been found out. But when Susan did neither of those things, Savanna's brows knit with confusion.

"I don't understand," she murmured to herself. "What happened to it?"

Now Daniel's mother frowned her own bewilderment. "What happened to what, dear?" she asked.

Savanna realized how wrong she'd been to think Susan would keep her letter of explanation from Daniel.

"I'm sorry," she said. "It's just that I sent the letter to your Fulton address. The house where you and your husband were living with Daniel. I hadn't been gone but a day or so before I sent it. And I thought that maybe...maybe you wanted to protect Danny. And that maybe you..."

Her voice was hollow and lacked resonance as she let the words trail off.

Susan quietly supplied the end of her thought. "That I hid your letter from him."

The woman's lips drew into the barest of smiles.

It was a smile of reassurance meant to let Savanna know that there was nothing held against her.

"I don't remember any..." She went quiet, then she went pale and pressed her hand against her mouth. "Oh, my," she said. "I do remember the letter." She reached over and took hold of Savanna's hand. "It arrived at such a terrible time. Daniel was so upset by your... leaving the way you did. He couldn't bear to be in the house. He couldn't bear to be outside. He didn't want to see anyone." She shook her head. "It was an awful time for him."

Savanna nodded her understanding. It had been an awful time for her too.

"Daniel decided to return to school early," Susan continued. "Several of his friends agreed to go along with him. To keep him company. They were all at the house, tossing duffel bags, gathering books, food and a million other things, trying hard to keep Daniel's mind off you and what happened. Those boys worked so hard to keep..." She smiled sadly.

Images ran through Savanna's head as she tried to imagine Daniel and his friends talking loudly, forcing their laughter in an effort to pretend that everything was normal.

"Anyway," Susan said, "when the mail was delivered, I handed your letter to Daniel. Everything stopped. The boys were totally silent as they waited for Daniel's reaction. He didn't hesitate a second before he gave me the letter, unopened, unread. He said he couldn't deal with it."

Her eyes became misty, her voice choked as she remembered her son's exact words and relayed them to Savanna. "He said, 'Mom, all I ever wanted was to see Savanna smile. If she's happy, then I can learn to live with this.'"

Susan Walsh sniffed and reached toward the end table to pluck a tissue from the box. She gently dabbed her watery eyes.

"I hurt him so much." It was painful for Savanna to get the words around the lump in her throat.

"If your letter had arrived a day earlier," Susan said, "things may have turned out differently. But as it was, Daniel just couldn't bring himself to face whatever was inside that envelope."

Savanna lowered her head as a heavy mantle of

guilt descended upon her shoulders. Daniel's mother squeezed her hand comfortingly.

"Just call it one of those twists I told you about," Susan said. "A sharp turn in the road of life that none of us can predict."

"I feel as though I swerved off the road and down the side of a steep cliff." Savanna accepted the proffered tissue from Susan.

"Now it's not as bad as all that."

Savanna looked pleadingly at the mother of the man she'd wounded so long ago. "Tell me how I can make him understand. Tell me how I can get Daniel to forgive me."

"Talk to him," came her simple answer.

"But he doesn't remember the letter," Savanna told her. "He doesn't know I tried to get in touch, tried to explain."

"Show him."

Savanna scanned Susan's face questioningly.

"I must have the letter someplace." Susan rose from the couch. "I can't imagine I'd have thrown it away. I'll be right back," she said, and then she left the room.

She was gone just a few minutes before she came

back carrying a large, white family Bible. Susan sat down and placed the book in her lap.

"I tucked your letter in here." She gently laid her hand on the leather bound cover "This is where I put so many important things. I guess I thought Daniel might change his mind and want to read it. But days and then weeks passed, and it completely slipped my mind." She opened the pages.

Savanna watched her sort through the hand-clipped obituary notices, school certificates, birth announcements and other personal mementos.

"I meant to wait awhile and then talk to him about it." Susan exhaled. "But then my husband passed. And then Celia found out she had breast cancer. I came here right away. And when she had the mastectomy I decided to move in to help her with the children." She looked beyond Savanna, her eyes clouding and added, "And now poor Celia is having such a rough time with her marriage."

Susan blinked and turned her regretful gaze back to Savanna. "I have to admit, I forgot all about your letter."

It was Savanna's turn to smile encouragingly. "It's okay," she assured Susan. "You were busy dealing with all the twists and turns in your own life. You couldn't be responsible for straightening out the ones in mine." Savanna's gaze dropped to the Bible in Susan's lap. "I do appreciate your keeping it, though."

Daniel's mother flipped a few of the pages and finally pulled out the white envelope, handing it to Savanna.

"Talk to him, Savanna," she said. "I know my son is as angry as a wounded bear. But if you can talk to him, I'm sure you can help him work it out." Susan closed the book's leather cover and looked down at her hands. "I just wish I could have spent more time helping him through his pain."

Realizing that the woman was regretting the fact that she couldn't be everything her children needed, Savanna reached out and hugged her.

"Talk to Daniel," Susan said, her gaze full of pleading. "I know you can help him."

Savanna tried to smile. "I will."

CHAPTER FIVE

———

"What do you want, Savanna?" Daniel filled the doorway of his home. His irritable countenance told Savanna in no uncertain terms that he was not happy to see her.

Tough, she thought. Meeting his gaze unflinchingly, she replied. "I want to talk."

"It's late," he said, the words short, terse. "I don't—"

She ducked under his arm and scooted into the house. She didn't wait to see if he turned to follow her; she was afraid if she didn't hurry through the foyer and into the living room he just might grab

———

her by the scruff of the neck and haul her back outside.

"Savanna!"

She ignored him, planted herself on the first available chair and waited for his entrance. He didn't disappoint her.

He came into the room, a frown biting deep into his forehead. "What the hell do you think you're doing?"

Compressing her lips, she fought the confident smile threatening to curl them upward. If she hadn't been clutching the unopened letter Susan Walsh had given her, Savanna felt she'd probably melt like hot jelly under those glinting eyes of his. But the envelope bolstered her confidence. This was her secret weapon. In fact, she had to fight the urge to wave it under his nose, taunting, "Neener-neener." She wouldn't flaunt it, though. She had made his mother a promise. A promise she intended to keep.

A blanket of solemnity settled over her and she said, "I really want to talk, Daniel." She looked at him and hoped her eyes and her tone conveyed the utter sincerity she felt in her heart.

When her statement did nothing to soften the

look he was leveling at her, she lifted her chin stubbornly and rephrased her intent. "I'm not leaving until we talk." She pressed her back against the soft cushion of the chair, folded her arms across her chest and waited for his response.

His eyes never left hers. His pupils were perfect black circles surrounded by irises that were brown, and dark, and hard. He stared at her for a long moment. Savanna refused to speak. She had all the time in the world.

Finally he relented. "So talk."

"This may take a while. You might want to sit down." She urged him with a coaxing smile.

"I'm fine right where I am." He planted his feet firmly on the carpet and tucked his hands deep into his trouser pockets.

She opened her mouth to insist, but decided against doing so. He wasn't going to budge, that much was apparent. She shouldn't argue. He'd met her halfway, he was willing to listen and for that she was grateful.

She unfolded her arms, her shoulders rounding softly. Leaning forward, she rested her hands lightly on her thighs. "I want to talk about what happened six years ago."

His eyes narrowed a fraction and his jaw clenched tight.

"Daniel, I mean it," she said firmly. "I'm not leaving until we talk this out."

He gazed up at the ceiling and massaged the back of his neck. He took a deep breath, and when next he looked at her, his gaze held a heavy mixture of resignation and dread. His mouth pulled into a dour line and he pushed his hands back into his pockets. "Okay, let's get this over with."

Looking up at him, Savanna suddenly felt at a loss. Where should she start? There was so much she wanted to say. Things she needed to say. She'd spent six years talking to an imaginary Daniel. During those lone conversations, she'd always been straightforward, very clear and concise with her explanations and her regret for having left him in the manner that she had.

Now that he stood in front of her, the only words that tumbled through her mind were gushing, apologetic phrases that would get them nowhere. Saying she was sorry might make her feel better, but she doubted that he was in any frame of mind to hear, let alone accept, a remorseful speech.

No, she had to take this slowly, methodically.

She had to make him understand her state of mind when she'd been nineteen. She had to make him realize how she had been feeling six years ago when she had run away from him, from their wedding, from their families and friends.

But before she did anything, she had to show him the letter. She had to make him see that she had tried to contact him, she had tried to explain. Doing so was the only way she would succeed in breaking down the wall of anger that he'd built. Only then could there be a hope of his actually absorbing what she had to say.

However, Savanna knew it was imperative that she prove her point gently. Her intention wasn't to make him feel badly or, heaven forbid, guilty. She didn't want to hurt him further. She only wanted to touch his emotions so that he'd listen. *Really* listen.

"Today," she began, "when we were in the park..."

His eyes closed. But she refused to let him shut her out.

"When we were in the park," she repeated louder, more firmly. "I told you I had written you a letter. And you said I hadn't."

He cocked his head to one side. "What you said was that you wanted to get in touch—"

"Daniel," she cut him off. "Let's not quibble over my exact words. The reason I brought up the subject earlier today was because I was trying to find some way to ask you why you never got in touch with me. Why you didn't answer my letter."

"I didn't answer your letter." His tone was as sharp as a well-honed blade "Because you never wrote one..."

She lifted her hand, and his voice trailed off, his eyes locking on the small, white envelope. His hands remained rooted deep in his pockets, but his gaze ricocheted from the letter, to her face and back to the letter.

"I went to see your mother this afternoon." Savanna's voice was barely a whisper. "She told me that my letter arrived the very day you went back to school."

She studied Daniel's face, hoping she'd sparked his memory. His eyes scanned the room, but she knew he wasn't seeing the deep-green upholstered couch, the cherry wood tables or the fox-hunting prints that hung on the wall. He was undoubtedly picturing in his mind events that took place years ago, events that had changed both their lives.

He lowered his eyelids. His chin tipped up and his shoulders relaxed. He gave a slow, tiny shake of his head. His exhalation was audible, and when he looked at her, his eyes were no longer hard and cold.

He nodded. "I remember."

Reaching out, he slipped the letter from her fingers. He sat down on the ottoman directly in front of her chair. His knee brushed against her thigh, but he didn't seem to notice. Savanna sat perfectly still, knowing from the look on his face that his mind was swimming with memories of that day.

"It all seems so long ago," he said, his eyes glued to the white envelope. "I was so confused. I felt... so angry with you. And I felt like my heart had been ripped out of my chest." He shook his head. "But the humiliation was the worst. To choose the one person in the world you want to spend the rest of your life with, and then have that person run from you the very day you'd planned to..." His voice broke and he stopped talking long enough to clear his throat.

Savanna let him take a moment to collect himself. He inhaled a deep, cleansing breath and then lifted his gaze to hers.

"I do remember getting the letter," he said. "I'd forgotten. I'm sorry I accused you of not sending it."

"I understand." Savanna tucked a strand of hair behind her ear. "Your mother said when the letter arrived you were with several of your friends. That the whole house was in an uproar. You were packing your things. She said...you told her you didn't want to deal with hearing from me."

"Couldn't," he corrected. "I *couldn't* deal with hearing from you, Savanna. You were safe. You couldn't have mailed a letter if you hadn't been. I assumed you were happy. You had what you wanted. That was all I needed to know."

"But my letter explained why I left..." Her voice faded when she saw him slowly shake his head.

"The 'whys' didn't matter. I didn't need to know your reasons."

"Of course you needed to know," Savanna insisted softly.

"Savanna," he said, staring at her steadily, "knowing why you ran off on our wedding day wouldn't have made me feel any less hurt, any less angry. Knowing why wouldn't have lessened my humiliation one iota." He signed. "The woman I loved didn't love me."

She gasped. "But that's not true."

Looking into his stony brown eyes, she knew he didn't believe her. And she realized just how badly her running away had injured him. Her gaze slid to the floor and she inhaled deeply, exhaled slowly.

Each time she had imagined explaining things to him, she'd always pictured him accepting her reasons. She had always been successful in conjuring a fantasy in which he would understand her motives. A fantasy in which he would, in the end, approve of her actions. But that's exactly what her imaginary conversations with Daniel had been... fantasies.

He was right in saying her explanation could never have eased his hurt and disgrace. The only thing she'd accomplished in sending the letter was instilling in herself a false sense of exoneration. All the guilt she'd ever felt about running away from him swirled around inside her chest, making her feel dizzy and sick.

She lifted her head and looked at him, a tear spilling over to trail down her cheek.

"I'm so sorry." Her voice was hoarse with emotion. She reached out and touched his knee. "Please, Daniel. I need you to forgive me."

He let the envelope flutter to the floor and he gently clasped her hand in both of his.

"Don't cry," he told her. "I never wanted you to cry." He gently squeezed her fingers. "It all happened a long time ago. It's over and done with."

"But it isn't over," she insisted. She sniffed. "Today when I tried to talk to you, I couldn't believe when you...I couldn't believe how you..." She couldn't even get the words out, and she had to press her lips together firmly to keep her chin from quivering at the memory.

"I know." His tone conveyed the depth of his regret for what he'd done to her. "I thought you were crazy when you accused me of being angry about something that happened six years ago. But..."

He rubbed his hands against hers and the friction of his skin on hers heated her chilled fingertips.

"My actions certainly spoke louder than my words, didn't they?" He grinned ruefully.

Savanna didn't say a word.

"I thought I had dealt with all those horrible emotions that were eating me up." He sighed. "I worked hard to crush them into what I thought was a neat little package that I stuffed into a box in the back of my brain."

Savanna slipped her fingers from the cradle of his hands and pressed her palm flat against his cheek.

"But, Daniel, don't you see?" she said. "Burying all those bad feelings didn't make them evaporate. They didn't go away. They only lay there festering, waiting to infect you again, waiting for something to trigger their poison."

"And you were the trigger."

She nodded. "I was the trigger." She let her hand drop to clasp his again. "And I don't think those emotions will ever go away until you deal with them, work through them." Her voice became small. "And I'm afraid the only way you can start is by forgiving me." She tilted her head. "Do you think you can?"

He looked away, rubbing his hand across his jaw.

"I thought I had," he said. "I really thought I had." When his eyes returned to her face they were anguished. "But my behavior today really showed me differently. That kiss should never have happened and I'm sorry."

"It's okay," she said. "It's okay because I understand what was happening, what you were feeling."

Daniel sighed heavily. "Maybe you're right," he said, reaching down and scooping up the letter that had fallen at his feet. "Maybe I do need to understand why you left. Maybe if you explained your reasons for bolting I could let some of this anger go." His gaze was piercing as he stressed, "I do want to let it go."

Steeling herself, Savanna assembled the words that she hoped would clearly express her rationale behind abandoning him on what should have been the most important day of both their lives.

"There was much more to my leaving," she began slowly, "than just the wedding. Ever since I was a child, I was taught to be good, listen to my elders, do what I was told. And in exchange, my parents coddled their perfect child, protected her, provided her with anything and everything she ever wished for."

Savanna noticed how she'd jumped to explaining in the third person, as though her childhood had happened to someone else. Somehow it was easier that way.

"Don't get me wrong," she said. "I'm not complaining. My adolescence was wonderful. I have beautiful memories of my childhood. Dad and mom were older when they had me. My mother told me a thousand times how long they'd waited for a child, and how happy they were when I was born. They wanted to give me everything they possibly could. The best of everything." She paused a long moment before divulging her disparagement. "But because my parents were so thorough in their providing for me, so extreme in their protecting of me, I never learned how to make choices. I never learned how to do things for myself. I was never given the chance."

She unlaced her fingers from his and flattened her palms on her thighs. "Mom and Dad provided me with every perfect thing. A perfect home, a perfect childhood, perfect schooling, perfect clothes..." Her eyes begged for his understanding of her next statement. "The perfect husband."

He was silent as he took in the implications of all that she said. Shaking his head, he asked, "Do I have this right? Running away from our wedding...running away from *me* was your way of rebelling against your parents."

"Well," she said, "I guess you could say I was rebelling against you too."

Daniel looked taken aback. "Rebelling against me for what? Loving you?"

"Of course not." she said. "Don't you see? It had nothing to do with how we felt about each other."

"I'm sorry," he said, pulling away from her. "But you've lost me."

"Ever since the first day we met, you took up where my parents left off." Savanna clasped her hands together. She was frightened that she would never make him understand. "You took up their cause. You told me what we were going to do and when we were going to do it. You wanted to know where I was and who I was with. Even when you were away at college, you called to make sure I was studying or if I needed help on an essay or working on this project or that one. You were as protective as my parents ever were."

"Because I loved you, for God's sake." He looked incredulous. "How was I supposed to treat you?"

"But, Daniel," she said, "I felt as though I was drowning in security, drowning in... love."

"Sounds like a fine way to go if you ask me," he said.

She reached up and massaged her temples and muttered, "I'm making an awful mess of this."

Lifting her gaze to his once more, she tried again to explain clearly. "It does terrible things to a person's self-esteem to think that everything must be decided for them. I started to think I didn't have the wits God gave a rock. I never had a chance to depend on myself. I never knew if I could."

She watched his gaze rove from her hair to her nose, mouth and chin, and then rise again to her eyes. When he spoke, his tone was as still and smooth as a glassy lake. "I did that to you?" he asked.

"It wasn't only you," she gently reminded him. And having heard an edge of guilt in his question, she said, "Besides, everything turned out fine. I turned out fine. Because I..." Her voice faltered.

"Because you ran away from me," he finished for her. "You ran away from what I was doing to you."

"Now, Daniel." Savanna lightened her tone in order to lift the dark mood that had descended on them. "You only treated me the way you thought I wanted to be treated. I didn't come home to explain all this so that you'd feel guilty. I only wanted to make you understand."

"Oh, I understand all right," he said softly. "You saved yourself. Do you realize that?"

Savanna's smile didn't quite reach her eyes.

"Your decision to leave town was a good one." He cocked his head and his eyes lit with a teasing glint. "I always wondered, though, why you waited to make that decision ten minutes before the wedding ceremony."

Slowly her cheeks flamed, and she grinned to hide her embarrassment. "My timing was awful, wasn't it? I've always felt badly about that." She shook her head, looking at him seriously. "How terrible was it for you?"

He shrugged. "I survived."

Her heart swelled with tenderness for him. His anger was dissolving. She knew it as sure as she knew her own name. Otherwise he wouldn't protect her from his bad memories by brushing off all that he'd gone through six years ago.

Daniel sighed and looked down at the letter he held in his hands. "Well, I guess you were right about everything. You showed me that I've been harboring a lot of bitterness and anger. And you made me understand that you had good reasons for leaving."

His lips tilted in a beautiful smile and his whole face transformed. She had always remembered Daniel as "the catch of the county" as Miz Ida had called him, but looking at him now, Savanna was awed by just how handsome he'd become.

"Do you mind if I keep this?" He indicated the letter he held.

"Of course not," she said, lifting one shoulder a fraction. "It's yours."

"I'll read it later." He stood and placed the envelope on the desk. Swiveling to face her, he said, "Savanna, I..." but his voice faltered before he could finish.

He seemed to be mulling something over, coming to some sort of decision. Through his facial expressions, she could see his mind churning. Finally he nodded slowly and lifted his gaze to hers.

"I have something," he said haltingly. "Something I'd like to return to you."

"To return?" she asked.

He nodded. "Stay right here. I'll only be a moment."

She listened as his footsteps faded down the hall, and wondered what he could possibly have that he would need to give back to her.

She stood to stretch out her legs. Savanna had to admit that she was pleased with their conversation. Things had been shaky at first, but all indications pointed to a nice smoothing out of the situation; she'd explained her reasons for running away and he seemed to accept them. Yes, everything was going to be all right.

Meandering around the room, she found herself in front of one of the matted hunting prints that hung on the wall. The foxhounds were so life-like, they threatened to jump right out of the heavy ornate frame. She studied the man in the picture, clothed in a bright red jacket and mentally substituted Daniel astride the roan mare. Savanna could see the sun glistening off the sweat-streaked flanks of the horse as Daniel commanded the animal using only the well-defined muscles of his thighs. Then she imagined those very same thighs, bare and pressed tight against hers. Her eyes fluttered closed as the fantasy took her hostage, and she was soon swamped in images of she and Daniel, both naked, hands smoothing over hot skin, lips touching, teasing, tongues tasting. Her heart skipped a beat at the wild, spontaneous vision that had seemed to come from nowhere.

"Lord," she murmured breathlessly, opening her eyes wide. What had prompted such an unrestrained image? Before she could gather her wits to come up with an answer, Daniel came into the room.

"Here it is," he said.

The sound of his voice and the very way he carried himself gave Savanna the distinct impression that Daniel was relieved about something.

He gingerly placed a small box on the palm of her outstretched hand.

"But before you open it," he said, "I have something I need to say."

Savanna pulled her hand closer to her chest and waited for him to speak.

After he took a deep breath, he quietly said, "Six years ago when you left..."

He looked deeply into her eyes.

"My life turned into a living hell."

A chill shivered up her spine, a chill that tingled all the way up the back of her neck and into her scalp. Hearing him say the words aloud filled her with a palpable guilt. She'd imagined he had suffered. She'd known she had caused him great pain. Even so, she wasn't prepared for his clear confirmation, and it was like a physical blow.

He must have noticed her despair, for he grasped her forearms and steadied her.

"Savanna, I'm sorry. I didn't say that to upset you. I only wanted..."

"It's okay." She swallowed hard and stepped away from him. "Please," she urged. "I want to hear what you have to say."

Daniel sighed audibly. His brown eyes were soulful, and looking into them, Savanna felt her heart would break.

"I was only trying to tell you..." He faltered. "I felt...rejected. The humiliation..." He shook his head. "I had never experienced anything like it before. It was... difficult for me. So difficult, in fact, that I never stopped to think what you may have been going through."

He ran an agitated hand over his lower jaw before he continued. "Anyway, I want you to know that I'm.. .letting all that go. I may not agree with the way you did things back then, but I do understand your reasons for leaving. And this—" he pointed toward the box she held to her chest "—is my way—" he gazed deeply into her eyes "—of forgiving you."

Savanna looked down at the small box in her hand.

"Go ahead," he said, "open it."

She lifted the lid and her throat immediately constricted with emotion, hot and thick. Unable to speak, she could only look with tear-blurred eyes at the tiny pearl buttons nestled inside. The tiny pearl buttons from her wedding dress.

CHAPTER SIX

———

"Thanks for coming to pick me up." Miz Ida said, closing the car door behind her. "Of course I'm perfectly capable of walking to the hospital, but it's nice to give these weary bones a rest."

"Weary bones," Savanna commented wryly. "You have more energy than I do. Anyway, there was no reason for you to walk when I was driving right by your place on my way to the board meeting."

"I'm glad you decided to come," Ida told her. "We could use some fresh ideas."

Savanna smiled in the fading light of the

summer evening. "Well, I'm sure full of ideas and I'm happy to help the hospital."

"I have the figures from the flea market," Ida said. "I'll be presenting them tonight. The Ladies didn't raise much money, but every little bit helps."

"The Ladies' Auxiliary organized a nice little gathering." Savanna glanced over and saw Miz Ida's humble shrug, but the woman was clearly proud of her efforts.

"I heard you had lunch with Daniel that day."

The statement came out of the blue, like a grenade lobbed into a crowd of innocent by-standers. Ida relished the surprise attack, that was certain. Savanna had to scramble to gather her wits.

"Um-hmm," she said.

"I also heard..."

Savanna's stomach tensed at Ida's probing tone.

"That things didn't end on a very good note between the two of you."

Feeling the need to stop the gossip about herself and Daniel from traveling any further along the grapevine, Savanna said, "Ida, Daniel and I did have words, I guess you could say. But I want to assure you, I've seen him since then and we've worked everything out. Things are fine between us. Just fine."

"Well, that's good," Miz Ida commented.

"In fact," Savanna continued, "I've seen him several times this week. He smiled. He waved. He even stopped and talked to me in a most friendly fashion when we happened to meet in the post office." She couldn't help overdoing it. She felt a desperate need to look out for her reputation. And Daniel's. Savanna raised a cocked eyebrow at Miz Ida. "I'm surprised you hadn't heard about that."

"Now don't go gettin' all bent out of shape," Ida said. "I only brought it up because Daniel is the attorney for the hospital. He's on the board, so he'll be at the meeting tonight. He'll get to vote on any ideas you bring up. And I'd rather not see you go into the meeting with one strike against you."

"I know that Daniel's on the board," she said. "And that shouldn't be a problem." Her tone was a little vague. She wasn't really worried that she'd be working with Daniel on this fund-raising effort. She *was* concerned to learn that stories were being passed around about the two of them. She was sure Daniel wouldn't like it, either.

As Savanna pulled her car into a parking space

in front of the hospital, she caught sight of Daniel walking toward the main entrance.

"I also wanted to know," Miz Ida started tentatively, "whether you were in a position to—"

"Just a minute." Savanna leaned toward her open window. "There's Daniel now."

This was a great opportunity to show Ida the friendly relationship she and Daniel shared. It just may put an end to all the talk. Honking the horn, Savanna waved furiously.

"Hello, Daniel," she called.

He lifted his hand in greeting, offered them a smile, and then disappeared into the building.

There, Savanna thought, if that doesn't show Ida nothing would.

Savanna opened her car door. "Let's get in there, Miz Ida. We don't want to be late."

She chose to ignore Ida's frustrated grumble. Savanna felt the woman would just have to deal with her disappointment regarding the rumors of trouble.

"I can't wait to present my ideas to the board," Savanna said as she pushed the button in the elevator that would take them to the third floor.

"Does everyone know I'm coming to give some input?"

Miz Ida hesitated before replying, "Most of them do."

Savanna felt a tingle of suspicion creep along her skin at the sound of Ida's guilty tone. "Most?" she asked.

"Well," Ida began, "I couldn't...I didn't know if... I wanted to wait and see..."

Squaring her shoulders and narrowing her eyes, Savanna turned to face Ida and said, "You didn't tell Daniel."

"Well...you see...I..." Miz Ida stammered. "It's not that I wasn't going to tell him at all. I simply didn't have the opportunity to do it."

"Right," Savanna said wryly. "Miz Ida, you not having the opportunity to relay some tidbit of information to someone is about as believable as the Statue of Liberty walking down Main Street."

Ida looked truly chagrined.

"He'll find out soon enough," Ida said. "Besides, if the two of you are on such friendly terms, then he won't mind in the least."

Savanna nodded her head with assurance. "He won't mind in the least."

Walking into the meeting room, she was surprised by how many people were in attendance. Miz Ida confirmed that many people of the community were concerned about the hospital and would be affected if the private establishment failed.

Several minutes were spent as Savanna greeted those citizens of Fulton she knew and was introduced to some she didn't. When Jim Thompson called the meeting to order, Savanna took a seat among the nonvoting attendants while Ida sat at her designated place at the long table in the front of the room.

The board discussed several different topics pertaining to the hospital and its employees' welfare. Savanna's attention slipped as her eyes were drawn to Daniel. He looked preoccupied, as though be might he upset by something. Maybe he'd had a rough day.

Savanna thought back to last weekend when they had had their talk. She'd been speechless when she'd opened the small box and seen that he'd kept the pearl buttons that she'd ripped from her wedding dress. As Daniel had explained how very hard it had been for him to face everyone that day, her heart had ached with empathy. He had gone on to describe the hellish few days he'd spent in Fulton until he'd finally had all he could take and decided to return to school early.

She had let him talk Sunday afternoon. Let him get it all out of his system. By the time she'd left Daniel's house, she felt they had come to a new understanding of each other. She was happy about that.

What she wasn't happy about, though, was the way Daniel kept coming to the forefront of her mind. Ever since their talk, she'd been bombarded with thoughts of him. Memories, old and new, continually flitted through her brain with no provocation whatsoever. And at night she was plagued by dreams, misty, erotic images that floated just out of her grasp with the dawning of the sun.

Savanna found herself looking for Daniel on her excursions into town, watching for him to drive by her house, hoping with each ring of the telephone that she would hear his voice on the other end of the line. She knew her behavior was ridiculous; he'd given no indication that he planned to see her or even contact her. But she watched and waited nonetheless.

It was becoming a problem. A problem she really didn't need. She knew she would...

"I'd like to present Ms. Savanna Langford."

The tail end of Ida Watson's introduction snapped Savanna to attention. She blinked and sat up straight.

"Come on up here, Savanna," Miz Ida called.

Picking up her briefcase, Savanna went to the front of the room. She placed her notebook on the table and took a seat.

"Everyone remembers Savanna, I'm sure," Ida commented. "I told you all that she offered to come and volunteer some of her time and expertise."

A muffled sigh erupted, and Savanna's eyes darted to Daniel's end of the table. Ida pointedly ignored the sound and continued talking.

"As you all know, Savanna is a professional fundraiser," Ida said, "and she's going to give us some ideas on how we can raise some money for the hospital."

Jim Thompson smiled a hearty welcome. "We're glad to have your help. Tell us what you have in mind."

After opening her notebook and scanning the page of notes she'd written, Savanna looked along the line of board members seated at the table.

"First," she said, "I'd like to let you know how pleased I am to be able to give something back to Fulton General. My father was given such expert care here when he fell off that ladder and broke his arm. And my mother wrote and told me how she wouldn't trust anyone but the doctors here to help her get her ulcer under control."

Savanna paused a moment. "The people at this hospital have taken care of the most important people in my life. Not only that, but the people who work here truly care about their patients. The nurse who cared for my father came to visit him at home after he was discharged. The ivy plant she brought him is still growing in the yard."

Her lips curled in a smile as she concluded, "I just want to let all of you know that I sincerely want to help Fulton General stay in business."

Her speech was met with enthusiasm and appreciation. Smoothing her hand over her notes, she cleared her throat and said, "Now let's get down to business. I've come up with several ideas that I think will work. The first is a carnival."

Savanna looked at the faces of the board members. "I've worked with two carnival owners in the past. Both offer something for people of all ages. There are kiddie rides for the younger children, faster rides for teens and everyone loves the games of skill and chance."

A murmur of approval rose from the people sitting behind her. The board members looked open to the idea. All but one. She couldn't stop to wonder why Daniel was so grim-faced.

"We pay the carnival owner a flat fee," she continued with her explanation, "and we raise the price of the rides to make a profit. And believe me, the profit is more than you might imagine. The last carnival I planned—

"It won't work." Daniel's voice was flat, emotionless.

She turned her head and their gazes collided.

"Why do you say that?" she asked.

"It sounds as though you should have been given a little more information."

Savanna could tell his sarcastic barb was directed at Miz Ida.

"More information?" Savanna kept her tone

light in an effort to hide the trepidation that
sprouted right in the area of her solar plexus.

Daniel glanced around the table and finally his
eyes clashed once again with hers.

"Since no one seems inclined to clue you in on
our little problem, I guess I'm the one who'll have
to pass on the bad news." He leaned toward the
table and rested his weight on his elbows. "We
have little to no working capital where this fund-
raising effort is concerned. And since booking a
carnival involves coughing up a hefty sum of
money..." He hesitated, looking for a reaction from
her.

Savanna could only nod. He was correct. Front
money was needed in order to get the carnival to
come to town.

He raised his chin and peered at her. "Then like
I said, it won't work."

She stared at him a long moment. It bothered
her that he seemed so pleased to have put an end to
the carnival concept.

"Well," Savanna started slowly. Then she looked
at Jim, the president of the board. "Is that true?"

Jim nodded solemnly. "I'm afraid it is."

The total failure of her first idea didn't bother

her as much as Daniel's strange demeanor. She hadn't expected his brusque behavior and she didn't know what was causing it. The worst thing was that she didn't have time to contemplate it, either.

"Okay," she said, thinking aloud, "then we need to keep it simple. How about using a telemarketing approach?"

She could see them waiting for her to explain. "This idea has no out-of-pocket cost, except for a few phone lines. And we already have those here at the hospital. We gather a few volunteers, make lots of calls, tell people our problem and ask for their help. Their monetary help."

"You mean beg?"

This time Daniel's tone held a hostile edge that was unmistakable.

Savanna looked him in the eye. "I'd prefer the phrase 'calling pleas,' or 'tele-petitioning.'"

"You just make that up?" he asked.

Was that a snicker she'd heard come from him? The anxiety she'd felt because of his questions now turned to ire. Why was he so set on negating every word that came out of her mouth?

"I'll have you know," she informed him, "that

this telemarketing angle has worked very well for me and my former clients in the past."

She glanced down the table, looking for some support. But everyone seemed content to sit and watch her and Daniel butt heads. Well, she had no intention of putting on a show for anyone.

"Fine," she said. "If that idea won't work for you..." she looked down at her notebook "...then how about a dinner? A big dinner. A grand, once-a-year gala of a dinner."

"How in the world could a dinner—" Daniel put special emphasis on the last word "—earn the kind of money we need to keep this hospital going?"

"You let me worry about that," she heard herself snap. She looked down at her notes and gritted her teeth. What was wrong with him? Why was he so hell-bent against every idea she suggested?

"Savanna?" Jim asked quietly.

She was relieved to give him her attention.

"Daniel has a legitimate question," he said. "It seems that a dinner would cost money, not make money."

Savanna straightened her spine. "Then I didn't explain myself very well. A fund-raising dinner can be a lot of work for a lot of people. But if it's put together correctly and managed well from the very start, then quite a lot of money can be made."

She named a figure and eyebrows shot up all the way down the table. All the way down to Daniel, that is. If he was impressed, he certainly was doing a fine job of hiding it.

"It just won't work" was all he said.

"Of course it will," she told him, her voice louder than she'd intended. She took a deep breath and added, almost plaintively, "If you'll give my idea a chance, you'll see."

What was she doing? She didn't need to grovel to him. There were fourteen other people on the hospital board. All she had to do was persuade them that she knew what she was talking about.

She made a point of avoiding Daniel's gaze altogether as she said, "This idea will work fine. If we can persuade area businesses to donate, or sell to us at cost, the supplies we'll need."

"How will we pay for these supplies?" Daniel asked.

Savanna didn't even glance his way when she answered. "Dinner tickets will cost five hundred dollars a plate."

Someone in the group behind her gave a surprised whistle.

She nodded. "That's how we make our money. And maybe we could have a head table for Fulton's most prominent citizens." She grinned wickedly "And we'll charge them a couple thousand. Maybe more."

"Dollars?"

The statement obviously boggled Daniel's mind.

"Yes," Savanna said. "You want to raise money, don't you? There's much more than just dinner taking place. That's why it's called a gala event. People dress to the nines. They come to see and be seen. The media will be out in force. People will see their names and pictures in local papers and a national magazine or two, if I can make that happen. And let's not forget the network news." Her tone was accusatory as she asked, "Daniel, wouldn't you cough up a few thousand dollars to save Fulton General?"

He ignored her question.

"The people of Fulton can't afford that kind of money," Daniel said. "You better take your fancy ideas back to the big city, Savanna."

His snide remark stung like a well-aimed slap.

A knee-jerk instinct compelled her to strike back. But she controlled her tongue. She refused to make a spectacle of herself in front of all these people.

Calmly she remarked, "There's no reason to stay in the confines of Fulton with our fund-raising efforts. People come from all over the county to be treated at Fulton General. We'll invite the Governor and the State Legislators. And there must be a Hollywood celebrity or two who own property in Virginia. If these people knew the hospital was in trouble, don't you think they would want to help?"

Her question raised a great deal of murmuring from the group behind Savanna and those sitting at the table. It was evident that the idea of petitioning the entire county, let alone the state, hadn't come up before now. Soon, no one speaker was leading the meeting as people talked out of turn, everyone discussing the merits of Savanna's ideas.

"Hold on just a minute." Jim Thompson tried to bring some semblance of order back to the meeting. "It seems as though we need some time to chew this over. Why don't we take a short break?

There are doughnuts and coffee on the table at the back of the room. Everyone, help yourselves."

As people gravitated toward the refreshments, Savanna made a beeline to Daniel.

"Could I speak to you a moment?" she asked him.

He nodded once curtly, then stood stock-still.

"Not here," Savanna said, nearly hissing the words. "In private."

She turned, went out the door and into the hallway. Although she couldn't actually see him, she sensed his commanding presence close on her heels.

Rounding a corner, she found an empty office and flipped on the light switch. She plunked her fist down on her hip and glared into his face.

"Well?" she asked.

"Well, what?"

"You know exactly what."

He simply folded his arms across his chest and leaned against the doorjamb.

"Great," she muttered. "Now you clam up. Listen, I want to know what's wrong with you. And I want to know now. I thought we worked all this out last Sunday night. I'm trying to help these people and you... you keep..."

"I keep what?"

"You keep knocking me down." She glared and waited for him to refute her accusation. When he did, she would have just the right words ready for him.

"What does our discussion Sunday night have to do with this fund-raising meeting?" he asked. "Come on, Savanna. Keep your arguments straight. We're either going to fight about one thing or the other."

The man was infuriating, the way he never said or did what she expected him to. In her frustration, she snapped, "Sunday night's discussion has everything to do with this meeting and you know it!" She pointed at him. "You say that you've forgiven me. You say that you've let go of your anger against me. But let's face it, you've shown here tonight that you haven't done either."

Daniel cocked his head, his brow furrowing. "Let me get this straight. You think that my being angry with you over something that happened six years ago has something to do with my finding fault with some of your fund-raising ideas?"

"*Some* of my ideas?" She was awed by his audacity. "I think your being against all of my ideas would have better explained what happened in there." She didn't wait for him to respond, but barreled ahead "And, yes. I think your anger toward me is keeping you from considering with an open mind anything I have to say."

When he spoke his voice was quiet. "The anger I *felt*." He stressed the past tense of the verb. "And that has nothing whatsoever to do with my negativity toward your efforts to help the hospital."

"What, then?" she asked, her tone clearly expressing the tension coiling inside her. "I'm committed to helping the hospital."

"I realize," he began, "that you think you're committed to the idea of helping us."

Savanna's brows drew together. "And what is *that* supposed to mean?"

Daniel sighed and raked his fingers through his hair. "I guess I didn't say that very well. What I meant was... I meant—" He stopped abruptly, shoved himself away from the doorjamb, and stood with his feet planted firmly apart. "Let's just stick to the original issue. My anger toward you had nothing to do with what went on in the meeting."

His hand began to bob as he punctuated each word. "You can believe me when I say I am not angry with you."

He seemed so sincere and that confused Savanna. If it hadn't been his anger, then what had made him so opposed to everything she'd said?

When it became clear that he had no intention of explaining himself without prompting, she asked, "Well, are you going to tell me what's going on in your head? I think I deserve to know why you were so antagonistic in there."

"You do deserve to know," he agreed.

The scowl on his face and the manner in which he jammed his fists into his pockets clearly told Savanna that he wasn't looking forward to saying whatever it was that was on his mind. As the eternity of one second ticked by, and then another, she had plenty of time to wonder what he was about to reveal.

Finally he simply shook his head. "There's no other way to say it but plain and clear." He looked her directly in the eye. "I don't want you to hurt these people," he said. "They know nothing about what goes into putting on a big, fancy dinner. This hospital, this town, means everything to them. I won't let you come in here, get their hopes high and then let them plummet to the ground." His dark eyes bore into has as he repeated, "I won't let you hurt these people, Savanna."

"Hurt them?' The question dripped with the incredulity that filled her to the brim.

His lips pursed tightly for a bare instant, then he spelled it out. "I don't trust you to stick around and see these high ideas of yours to fruition."

His words slowly settled into her brain. She felt as though her heart was in a vise, and his cutting accusation turned the lever, tightened the squeezing pain.

When she spoke, her voice was tiny, wounded. "I won't back out on these people. I'd never do anything to hurt them."

His gaze didn't soften. "You would never intentionally hurt them. But you'll hurt them just the same."

The white line around his compressed lips silently shouted out to her that he knew this from experience. Personal experience. God, would she never be able to live down the fact that she'd run out on him?

"This is a worthy cause and I know you mean

well." He stepped close to her and put his hands on her shoulders. "But you and I both know that the minute something doesn't go your way, or you find another more worthy cause somewhere else, or if the impulse strikes, you'll fly out of here like a bird on the wind."

Savanna's breath was knocked out of her just as if he'd hit her in the stomach. She couldn't believe what she was hearing.

"It wasn't like that before," she said. "I didn't leave six years ago because something didn't go my way." As she repeated his words, their meaning suddenly smacked her in the face. He thought she was irresponsible, and that sparked a fire in her. "I didn't run away because of some cause!" Her voice rose in volume. "And the urge to leave town didn't just strike me out of the blue."

She looked into his eyes and realized that they both knew her last statement wasn't true. Knocking his hands off her shoulders, she backed up a step. She needed some room to breathe, to think.

"You don't understand at all why I left, do you?"

He folded his arms across his chest and quietly said, "I understand perfectly why you left. You had legitimate reasons, wonderful reasons." The muscle in his jaw tensed. "When the people of Fulton need you to come through for them..."

Like I once needed you to come through for me, his eyes conveyed.

"...you'll find other reasons to leave. Just as legitimate. And in your mind, just as justifiable."

She refused to be hurt by his distrust. And she tried hard to fight against the ire building inside her, but she couldn't keep her eyes from narrowing the tiniest bit as she said, "You can't keep me out, Daniel. This is my hometown. I know these people. I will help them. No matter what you say. I will."

Shoving past him, Savanna stomped down the hall toward the meeting room. She paused at the closed door when she heard hoopla and applause coming from inside.

Daniel came up behind her and, reaching around her, turned the knob and pushed open the door.

"Well, that's it, then," they both heard Jim Thompson say. "Meeting adjourned."

"What's going on?" Daniel's question dampened the happy atmosphere of the small crowd.

Jim looked surprised. "Daniel, Savanna. We couldn't find the two of you," he said. "Ida said that you had probably left."

Daniel glared at Miz Ida, who had sense enough to avoid his eyes.

"We discussed a couple of Savanna's ideas," Jim went on. "We took a vote."

Savanna felt a flutter of excitement wash over her.

"Don't look so dour, Daniel," Ida said. "The board had a quorum present. And we all knew how you felt about Savanna's ideas. Your thoughts were taken into serious consideration."

Jim looked at Savanna. "Of course, the carnival was voted down," he said. "Simply because we don't have the front money to make it happen."

Daniel's smug "harrumph" behind her made her want to plant a well-aimed elbow in his ribs.

"But I'm happy to tell you that both the telemarketing idea and the gala dinner were unanimously approved." Jim smiled and shook her hand. "I hope you're ready to work for Fulton General, because we have lots of volunteers but absolutely no experience. It's going to be like teaching a group of babies how to walk."

"Don't worry, Jim," Savanna was quick to assure him. "I'll be here every step of the way."

She could barely contain herself. She wanted so badly to turn around and thumb her nose at Daniel. He didn't believe in her, but these people did.

"Oh," Miz Ida piped in, "the room we're planning to use to make the phone calls only has two telephones, so the board members paired off." She smiled sweetly. "Since you weren't here, Daniel, we matched you with the expert." Ida glanced from Daniel to Savanna and back to Daniel.

Savanna felt a giggle bubble at the back of her throat, but she held it in check. This was a perfect opportunity to show Daniel that she really intended to come through for the people of Fulton.

Before he could object to working with her, she turned to face him and said in a rush, "I'm free any night you are, Daniel."

CHAPTER SEVEN

"Daniel's leaving Fulton?"

Jolted by Ida's disclosure, Savanna stared, wide eyed. Finally she shook her head. "It can't be true. Daniel wouldn't leave town. Why would he do such a thing? How do you know this? Who told you? When did you hear this?"

"Whoa," Ida said. "Just slow down and let me talk a minute. This isn't idle hearsay."

Savanna accepted her change from Ida and tucked it in her wallet.

"My cousin Emma's daughter does some typing for Daniel's office manager when things get busy," Ida explained, bagging up the groceries. "Emma called me, all upset, and told me that Darlene had typed and mailed a letter that Daniel had dictated into his little recorder machine. She said that he was sending for information about a partnership offer. An offer from a big law firm in Richmond."

Ida fell silent, and Savanna spent an inordinate amount of time rooting in her purse for her keys as she tried to take in the information.

This just didn't make sense. Why would Daniel even think about leaving Fulton? This was his hometown.

"It was Emma's opinion..." Ida's voice broke the stillness that had fallen over them like a pall "...that his reason might have something to do with you."

"But that's ridiculous," Savanna exclaimed. "How on earth could it have anything to do with me? I haven't been here for years, and I'll be gone this time next month..."

As the words faded, she realized that she may not be telling the honest truth. She had to admit that staying in Fulton, moving her base of operations here, had crossed her mind. The friendliness of this small town, the place where she was born, had raised a longing in her. A longing to come home.

"I know," Ida said. "I told Emma that. But from what she said Darlene said about that letter, Daniel is dead serious." She gazed at Savanna with troubled eyes. "And if he does leave town, Fulton will be losing someone special."

* * *

"I just can't understand it," Savanna said as she strolled along the sidewalk with Amanda in tow.

Sheila absently rubbed the small of her back. "Something is weighing on his mind. Something heavy. Otherwise I'm sure Daniel would never consider leaving town."

"He's the hospital's attorney," Savanna replied more to herself than to Sheila. "Doesn't he know how much those people need him? Especially now when things are so bad at Fulton General."

"Jimmy, get back up on the sidewalk," Sheila warned her son. "It's not safe to walk in the street."

"Aw, Mom." Jimmy reluctantly stepped up onto the curb.

"Have we walked too far?" Savanna asked Sheila.

"No." Sheila smiled. "I'm fine. Let's go one more block and then we can head for home."

Amanda hopped over the cracks in the sidewalk.

"Step on a cwack, bwake your mommy's back," the little girl sang.

"I was just so surprised yesterday," Savanna said, returning to the original topic, "when Ida said I might be the reason Daniel is thinking about leaving.

Sheila shrugged. "Well, you did say you may have given him the impression that you'd like to move back to town."

"I've hinted, I guess." Savanna grimaced. "I guess you could say that I've dropped hints to everyone I've met.' She tucked a strand of her hair behind her ear. "Mostly in way of compliments. Everything feels clean and fresh here. Homey. The people are friendly. Neighborly would describe it better, I think, and I've commented about these things to everyone. I hadn't realized it, but my subconscious has been talking since the day I drove into town."

The smile that tilted Sheila's lips was warm. "You really do want to come home, don't you?"

Savanna hesitated, started to speak, then pressed her lips together. She couldn't even think about that right now.

"We really should do something about Daniel," she said.

Sheila slowly shook her head. "No, we shouldn't."

"What do you mean? I'm seeing him tonight at the hospital. We're making calls for contributions. I can ask him about it. Tell him what I heard."

"Savanna." Sheila stopped her ebullience with a frown. "He needs to work this out for himself. I know your first instinct is to pounce on him and confront the issue. That's your way of doing things. But it's none of your business. It's none of my business."

"But..."

"No 'buts,'" Sheila said. "I really think everyone should leave Daniel alone. Miz Ida included. I know her worries are plastered with good intentions. But if and when Daniel wants us to know his plans, he'll tell us."

"But he may be leaving because of me," she stressed.

"If you move back to town," Sheila commented, "Daniel will have to learn to live with it."

"Or move out of town and not live with it," Savanna muttered.

"Either way." Sheila said with finality, "he should be allowed to make his own decision."

Rounding the corner in silence, they headed back toward their street. Inhaling deeply, Savanna tipped her chin and felt the warm sunlight on her face, listened to the birds singing in the trees above her head. She thought it ironic that she was thinking of coming home to Fulton and Daniel was thinking of leaving.

She wouldn't want anyone telling her what she should or shouldn't do. Who was she to question Daniel about considering a move to Richmond? His mother lived there. So did his sister, Celia, and her family. And if he had been offered a lucrative business partnership, then that was only one more incentive for him to go.

Turning to Sheila, she said, "You're right. Daniel has a lot to work out. And none of it has anything to do with me. I won't ask him about it." A grin forced its way across her mouth. "No matter how much I might want to."

* * *

Savanna brushed her hair until it was soft and smooth. The weight of it fell across her bare shoulders. Slipping her arms into the royal-blue silk shell, she pulled the top over her head and flipped her hair out from the rounded neckline.

The supple fabric felt sensuous against her skin as she tucked it into the waistband of a pair of body-hugging black trousers. She slipped her black-stockinged feet into black leather flats and stood in front of the full length mirror to look at herself.

"My, my, my," she said, pleased with the image staring back at her. She fastened a simple gold chain around her neck and gold hoop earrings into her earlobes. A touch of lipstick and a swipe of mascara and she'd be ready.

The thought of seeing Daniel tonight brought a tickle of excitement to her stomach. And she wanted very much to look exceptionally good. She knew the two things were very much connected. It bothered her that since she'd returned to Fulton, Daniel hadn't stopped accusing and preaching at her long enough to notice that she was a real flesh-and-blood person, a real flesh-and-blood woman. She wanted to change that.

Being noticed by men had never been a problem for Savanna. In fact, the problem had been the opposite. Her public-oriented occupation had been the cause of all the male attention she received, she was sure.

Having a job that required constant contact with so many people, it was only natural that men would ask her out. She'd always made it a rule to be up-front and honest with the men she chose to date. And she'd tried hard not to hurt the few who had become serious about her.

But in all the six years since she'd left Fulton, she'd never found a man who conjured the kinds of physical reactions in her that Daniel had. She'd worried that she'd somehow made more of her relationship with Daniel than what it had really been. She worried that, in her mind, she may have turned what she and he had shared together into some kind of fantastic, intimate fantasy, the likes of which she'd never again find.

And here she was, taking great pains to look attractive, going out of her way to make certain that Daniel would become aware of her as a woman. Why? she wondered, looking closely at her reflection in the mirror. Why would she want to attract the attention of a man she hadn't seen in so long, a man whom she had hurt and humiliated, a man who had made it clear that he wanted nothing to do with her?

A shocking answer to the question flitted at the edge of her thoughts, causing a flush to creep over her skin. She shook her head sharply and pushed the entire train of thought from her mind.

Making Daniel notice her should be the least of her worries. She should be thinking of the fund-raising dinner, of the plans that were still left to be made. There were plenty of them. She should be focusing on updating the schedule she'd made for the volunteers who were willing to make telephone calls for contributions that would benefit Fulton General.

She grabbed her purse and her satchel and went out the door. Tonight she was going to teach Daniel the fine art of telemarketing. For now, she needed to focus on that fact alone.

With fund-raising plans whirling in her mind, she pulled the car out of the driveway and steered toward the hospital. A dark foreboding descended on her as she drove through the streets of this small town. What if Daniel was right? What if her ideas were too much for the people of Fulton? Could she handle this job competently? There were so many people in the community depending on her. Would Daniel's prediction come true? Was there any possibility of her getting scared or overwhelmed or who-knows-what and leaving before seeing the dinner complete and successful?

The questions tied knots of doubt in her stomach. A tiny frown pulled her brows together. She was letting Daniel's pessimism color what she knew about herself. She wasn't that frightened teenager any longer. Never had she let down a client. Not even once had she met with anything but success since she'd started her business. Raising money was a talent, a skill she'd honed to perfection. She was more than capable of handling this job. And she'd be damned if she'd let Daniel Walsh make her feel otherwise.

After she parked the car and slammed the car door shut, she squared her shoulders with a fierce determination and marched toward the hospital. She would see that this dinner was a success. She would make sure that the volunteers raised more money for Fulton General than they had ever imagined. If Daniel thought differently—and she knew that he did—well, he'd best get ready to learn that Savanna Langford didn't back down until she accomplished her goal.

She found the office that was set up for the purpose of making telephone calls. The sight of Daniel sitting at the lone desk, impatiently tapping a pencil against a yellow legal pad caused a seed of anxiety to sprout in her.

"Am I late?" she asked.

He lifted his head. "No," he said. "I was early."

She set her briefcase on the desk, opened it and extracted a notepad and pen.

"I'm sorry about the close confines," he said, waving a hand to indicate the small room. "It's the only office not in use."

"It's okay," she said, her tone clipped. "We don't need anything elaborate to get the job done. A couple of telephones. A quiet room where we won't be disturbed." She eyed her notes and then him across the desk. "Since I only have one copy of notes, how about if I come around there and we can share?"

The thought of sharing anything with Daniel brought an unexpected rush of heat to her cheeks. She dipped her head, letting her hair fall in a curtain that covered the side of her face, and rummaged in her satchel in an effort to hide her reaction.

"Sure," he said.

He stood, slid his chair to one side and came around the desk to pick up the other chair.

"I can do that," she told him.

"And what would my mother say about the manners of a Southern gentleman who allowed a lady to carry her own chair?"

His easy grin caught her unawares, and before she realized it, her own lips were drawn back in a warm smile.

"You're right," Savanna commented. "She wouldn't take too kindly to that idea."

"There you go." Daniel set the chair into place and gestured for Savanna to sit.

She did, and as he settled into his chair she said, "She looked good, by the way. Your mother. When I visited her last week, I was happy to see her healthy."

Daniel nodded. "I wish I had the time to visit her a little more often than I do."

Is that why you're thinking of leaving Fulton? The question was on the tip of Savanna's tongue, but she refused to ask it.

She glanced at her wristwatch. "We really should get started," she said. "I need a few minutes to explain how this works before we can begin making calls. And we don't want to call anyone much later than eight o'clock."

Daniel glanced at the notepad that she'd placed between them. He listened to her explain the procedure, but his eyes were riveted to her fingers as they lightly grasped the pen. Her long, perfectly tapered nails were coated with a dusky-pink polish, the skin of her hand smooth and pale. He imagined those fingers playing over his arms, his chest.

Stop it! He commanded himself. The same sort of wild images had plagued him the evening of the last hospital board meeting. He'd hardly been able to pay attention to the business being discussed with Savanna sitting in the room. And when she'd approached the table of board members to explain her fund-raising ideas, the sultry pictures in his brain had intensified. He'd had to physically push them out of his mind and concentrate on foiling her plans of joining the fund-raising team.

He'd hated to hurt her feelings. And he knew he had when he'd come right out and told her that he didn't expect her to hang around long enough to complete any project she might start. But he'd felt it was imperative to be honest.

The rumor floating around town was that Savanna wanted very much to come home for good, to move back to Fulton. She'd said something about it to him. But he'd also heard from her own lips that she planned to return to Baltimore in a few short weeks. Would she stay or would she go? Who could say for sure? How could she commit herself to helping the hospital when she was so damned flighty and indecisive? Thinking of her capricious nature only made him glad he'd had sense enough to keep all his options open by querying the Richmond law firm.

The townspeople didn't know Savanna the way he did. He was certain that she was going to start the ball rolling on this big dinner project, and then she'd abandon the very people she was supposed to be helping. Whether she high-tailed it back to Baltimore or just quit the plans to go dance in the sun, either way she'd leave a mess that none of the folks in Fulton were prepared to handle.

Well, he would have to keep a close eye on all of Savanna's plans. That way he'd be better prepared to pick up the pieces when she left. Better prepared than he'd been the last time she'd run off.

"Prepare yourself," Savanna said.

The words sent a chill racing along Daniel's spine. He lifted his head to stare into her clear, blue eyes.

"More people will hang up on you than will listen to what you have to say." She tapped the end of the pen lightly on her chin. "If you can keep the potential contributor's attention for the first fifteen seconds, then you've got a live one. The longer people listen, the more likely they will be to contribute."

"I see," he said.

She scooted her chair closer to the desk. "Well, let's give it a try."

Realizing that he'd become so caught up in his thoughts that he hadn't heard a word she'd said, he quickly gazed down the list of pointers from which she'd been reading. "If you'd like, I'll make a couple of calls and you can listen to my end of the conversation," she offered.

"Sounds like a good idea."

He watched Savanna dial the first name on the list the hospital administration office had supplied.

"Here goes," she whispered.

Her voice was warm and friendly as she explained who she was to the person on the other end of the telephone line. As the seconds ticked by and the one-sided conversation became more animated, Daniel knew that Savanna had what she'd called "a live one."

Daniel focused on her mouth when she chuckled lightly into the receiver. Her strawberry-colored lips pulled into a lingering smile that caused his blood to heat. She stared across the room, immersed in her discussion.

He had to admit that she knew how to play on the prospective donor's ego. People liked to be appreciated; further more, people liked for others to know of their generosity. Why settle for the silver club when one could become a member of the gold club, or even better, the platinum club. And everyone in town would see the names of each club's members in the pamphlet that would be printed after the fund-raiser ended. Man, she was good at this.

He rested his elbow on the table, curled his fingers and rubbed the backs of them across his chin, using quick, short strokes. Her blue eyes fascinated him...had always fascinated him. He remembered years ago how he could make them shine with giddy excitement when he brought her some small surprise or other, and how he could make those same eyes darken with desire until they were as deep and soft as navy-hued velvet.

The muscles low in his gut tightened as the memories bombarded his brain.

"Ooo-Wee," Savanna exclaimed as she replaced the telephone receiver into its cradle. "Fifty dollars!" She marked the amount down beside the caller's name. "Did you hear that, Daniel? Fulton General is fifty dollars richer after just one phone call."

There, he thought, those blue eyes of hers were shining with excitement just as he remembered. He was helpless against the next question that entered his head...could he make those eyes darken with desire?

As if by its own volition, his hand reached out and he gently stroked her silky blond hair. Then the backs of his fingers grazed her cheek.

"You're beautiful when you smile," he murmured.

She froze for a mere instant. The excitement

that had danced in her eyes a moment before changed to an inquisitive gleam. Then she smiled again, just for him. A slow, languorous smile that tempted and teased.

"Thank you," she said.

Without even thinking about his actions, Daniel ran his fingers along the length of her jaw, over her chin and rested them on the pulse point of her throat. He felt the blood throb through her veins, the pulsing causing his own heartbeat to quicken.

"You've changed."

Savanna grinned. "For the better, I hope."

He could only nod, thinking it ungentlemanly to explain. But in his mind he noted how the teenage Savanna he'd known six years ago had had a rounder face and a body that had been rail thin. Time had altered her, thinning out her face to define high cheekbones and a delicate jaw, and filling out her body with lush, irresistible curves. He was afraid she wouldn't appreciate his opinion of how she'd changed, but he certainly liked what the years had done.

"I think it's only fair to tell you," she said, her voice whisper soft, "that I wanted you to notice."

Her cheeks tinged a gorgeous pink and he enjoyed watching her become flustered.

"I mean, I wanted you to see that I was a woman."

The color in her face deepened as her embarrassment escalated. She shook her head.

"What I meant to say was that I wanted you to see me as someone other than the teenager from your past..." Her voice trailed and she dipped her head, turning away from him.

Lifting her chin with his index finger, he looked into her eyes and assured her, "I know exactly what you mean."

"I feel like I'm all of sixteen," she muttered.

Daniel had to chuckle. "Me too."

He smoothed a trembling hand over her shoulder and reveled in the feel of the soft silk of her blouse. He'd sell his soul right now to feel the silkiness of her skin beneath it.

His breath caught in his throat as the muscles in his lower abdomen began to ache. He hadn't felt desire this strong in a very long time.

Locking onto her gaze, he watched her eyes darken to the deep-blue color of a southern twilight. Was that an invitation he saw there?

"May I kiss you?" The question sounded almost too formal even to his own ears, but he needed to be sure.

The merest hint of a smile parted her full, sultry lips. "Please."

He continued to stare a moment longer. The problems and doubts that faced them outside the door would still be there when they emerged from this small office. He hadn't a single qualm about that. And his rational mind told him to stop this, here and now, before it went any further. However, right now his mind was anything but rational. It wasn't his mind he was listening to, anyway.

All he wanted was to taste Savanna's lips, smell the secretive scent of her skin, feel the softness of her hair brush his cheek. All he wanted was to spend a few moments lost in the desire she roused in him.

For an instant, he pondered pulling away, denying the need that called, no, screamed inside him. But then she touched him, her warm, sure fingers gliding over the back of his hand and wrist, along his forearm...and he was lost.

He lowered his head, ever so slowly, and pressed his lips against the curve at the base of her neck.

Nibbling his way up to her ear, he inhaled deeply the scent of her hair and a picture of a flowery meadow came to his mind. He kissed the sensitive skin behind her ear and her sharp intake of breath nearly made him smile. He remembered the spot as being one of her erogenous zones, and joy burst through him knowing he could still draw that kind of reaction from her.

Pulling her to him, he slid his hands around her back and hugged her tightly. She felt good in his arms. So very good.

He was only momentarily surprised when she raised herself a scant inch, eased her weight from her chair and slid onto his lap. She settled in, burying her face in the crook of his neck.

Heat flowed through his veins as though his blood was liquid fire. Savanna stoked the flame when she touched her lips to his neck. Her mouth felt cool and moist. And when her tongue flicked out to taste him, his breath quickened.

Pulling her back gently, he rained small, soft but urgent kisses all along her jawline. He tasted her pert chin and then kissed his way to her other ear. Nipping her earlobe with his teeth, he then soothed it with his tongue. She arched her back and shivered deliciously.

He lifted his head and darted a glance at her face. Her closed eyes, fanned with dark, delicate lashes. Her full mouth, ripe and ready and waiting. Her milky skin, flushed from his kisses.

Her eyelids fluttered open. She stared at him with irises that were a familiar deep navy. Again, emotion coursed through him, hot and strong, at the knowledge that he had aroused the desire he read in her gaze. The realization came to him slowly that she had the material of his shirt bunched in her fists.

"Dear, God, Daniel." Her words were a throaty whisper. "Kiss me."

Swallowing hard, he tried to get a grip on himself. His gaze searched hers until her eyes cleared a bit.

"What are we doing?" he asked, his voice hoarse.

"I don't know," she told him. Her tone was erotically breathless. "Right now I don't care. I don't want to think about it."

"Then we won't."

After six long years, he covered her lips with his.

CHAPTER EIGHT

———

Savanna hummed as she rolled paint onto the wall, using long strokes to turn the beige guest room a bright, cheery white. She was surprised by the small amount of paint it was taking to cover the walls. Once the paint dried, she'd hang the green chintz curtains she bought, toss the new throw pillows she'd found on the bed, and the bedroom would have a fresh, new look.

Stepping back from the wall, she took a moment to rock her hips to the soft pop music floating from the radio. She sang a line of the song and ended up in a fit of laughter remembering how, as a child, she had overheard her music teacher remark that "little Savanna Langford couldn't carry a tune in a bucket." The woman had been right, Savanna thought ruefully, but that didn't keep her from singing.

Lord, she was happy. Plans for the fund-raising dinner were going better than she could have expected. And the volunteers reported that their telephone pleas were being met, for the most part, favorably which meant profitably. Although she'd had to take some gentle ribbing from Miz Ida. The woman was the only board member to point out that the night Savanna and Daniel had been scheduled to make telephone calls, there had been only one pledge made. Savanna had tried to explain how she and Daniel had become busy talking, catching up after six years, but she was certain Ida hadn't believed a word she'd said. Savanna tingled from her head to her toes just thinking about that night. Daniel's kiss had been worth every bit of teasing Miz Ida could dole out.

The main reason for the happiness trilling inside her, Savanna knew, was the fact that she'd had dinner with Daniel three nights running. Oh, there hadn't been another passionate encounter such as the one they'd shared in the office at the hospital. But nowhere was it written that she couldn't hope. Savanna laughed aloud, the sound echoing off the bare walls.

She thought Daniel might call her a little later. Maybe she could suggest they go to the movie theater on Main Street. Then, she mused, maybe he'd walk her home in the romantic moonlight. Maybe they would take a shortcut through the park. A sensual smile lingered on her mouth and a chuckle rumbled deep in the back of her throat. Maybe they would find that park bench, the same one they'd shared on their first date, the same one where they shared their first kiss.

The giddy feeling that tickled through her made her press her palm flat against her stomach. She felt like a teenager again. Life was perfect. Well, nearly so.

There were a couple of small clouds throwing shadows over her exhilaration. Daniel still believed that she was going to leave the hospital in a lurch. Oh, he didn't say the words out loud. He didn't have to. She saw the guarded look in his eyes when the topic of the dinner came up. They worked hard to avoid talking about the fund-raising activities.

And then there was the continued rumor of his

leaving Fulton. Ida's Cousin Emma had reported that Darlene had heard that the senior partner in the law firm located in Richmond had called Daniel several times. Savanna wondered why he hadn't said anything to her about his plans.

Bending over, she turned up the volume of the radio. She'd play the ostrich, she decided, and hide her head in the sand a while longer. That was the only way she could go on seeing him and not confront him with the gossip and questions she had about his partnership offer. And if there was one thing she knew, it was that she had every intention of continuing to spend time with him. Indeed, she did.

As she belted out another off-key chorus of the song, she scooted her roller into the tray until it was saturated with white paint. Stretching her arm high, she smoothed paint to the wall.

The sound of a single tap caught her attention. She stopped painting and looked toward the door. Then she heard another tap. And another. When she realized the sound was coming from the window, actually the sound was caused by something hitting against the glass, she put down the paint roller and leaned to look through the screen.

Daniel was standing in the backyard, a fistful of tiny pebbles in his hand. His lips were moving, but she couldn't hear him.

"Just a second," she called. "Let me turn down the radio." When she returned to the window, she asked, "What were you saying?"

"I said, turn down the radio," he yelled.

Savanna laughed. "Come on in."

"I tried, but the door's locked."

"I'll be right down."

Padding down the stairs in bare feet, Savanna tucked the extra-wide neck of her big, comfortable t-shirt back onto her shoulder and tugged at the frayed hem of her tight denim cutoffs. Then she smoothed her hand over her bangs and fingered the red print bandanna she'd used to tie her hair up into a ponytail.

She grinned ruefully and thought, *You can't expect to look the glamor girl every time you see him.*

"Hi," she said, stepping back from the open door.

"Hi, yourself."

He brushed his lips against her cheek. Once they

separated, she could tell by the way he avoided her eyes that he was as startled by the impulsive kiss as she.

Reactive emotions swirled in her at a dizzying speed. Lord, a simple kiss shouldn't cause her such havoc. Inhaling deeply, she smiled and took the piece of paper Daniel held out to her.

"I stopped in at Ida's store," he said. "She mentioned that she had this list for you, and when she found out I was coming over she asked me to bring it along."

He spoke quickly, almost nervously, as though be felt he might need an excuse to visit her.

Feeling the urge to rib him a little, she made her voice sweet and innocent as she said, "You were coming over?"

Daniel actually blushed. Shrugging, he explained, "My afternoon appointment canceled and I thought..."

She couldn't hold her laughter any longer. Finally recognizing her teasing for what it was, he shot her an embarrassed grin and shook his head.

"Didn't your mother ever teach you that it's not nice to poke fun at people?"

Placing a hand on his forearm, she said, "You don't need an excuse to come here."

Glancing at the paper he'd handed her, she squealed and jumped into the air.

"This is the list of caterers Ida promised me," she said. "I can't wait to get started calling them." She looked into his face. "The dinner plans are going so well, Daniel."

The aura of boyish charm that had surrounded him a split second earlier dissolved before her very eyes. His gaze, although not exactly hard, no longer twinkled with openness and friendship. His whole demeanor turned cautious and restrained, and she hated this seemingly unscalable mountain that suddenly separated them.

"I'm sorry," she mumbled, fighting the part of her nature that screamed for her to confront him. "Let me just put this on my desk. I'll look at it later." She turned and took a step toward the den.

"No. Wait."

Daniel's quiet voice stayed her.

"I'd like to hear what's been happening with your plans," he said.

She didn't miss his choice of pronouns. When he'd spoken to her of the hospital budget difficulties, he'd used the phrase "our problems." But when it came to her ideas for a solution, he used the description "your plans." He separated himself. Maybe not consciously, but he separated himself nonetheless. And Savanna couldn't deny that it hurt.

His asking for an update on the fund-raising dinner, however, did lighten her spirit a little. Maybe there was light at the end of the tunnel, even if it was dim.

"Well," she began, "we booked the country club. And the manager called me just yesterday with news. They've decided to donate the use of the club." She couldn't help her wide smile. "I'm so excited. That means we don't pay a penny."

Absently she hitched the neckline of her T-shirt back onto her shoulder. "The tickets are being printed as we speak. Free of charge, I'm proud to add. And I've contacted three florists, all of whom have offered to donate flowers. I've promised to print the names of all contributing businesses in the program and mention them to any newspapers considering a write-up about the dinner."

"That sounds great."

Savanna tried to ignore the fact that his smile didn't quite reach his eyes.

"And now," she went on, "Ida's come up with a list of caterers in the area. I can't expect to get the food free, but I'll do what I can to keep costs as low as possible. The lower the overhead, the more profit for the hospital."

Watching his jaw muscles work, she thought, *He has so little trust in me.* If she could only make him see...

"Daniel...I wish there was something I could say..."

But there wasn't. Trusting her was something he had to learn on his own. The realization made her spine straighten. It was so true. Nothing she could say would make one iota of difference. Daniel had to learn he could believe in her all by himself. All she could do was continue to pursue her goal, continue to work toward overcoming Fulton General Hospital's problem. And hope that Daniel realized she was worthy of his trust.

"Something you could say about what?" he asked, unaware of or unwilling to admit that she realized just how uptight he was.

She shook her head. "Nothing." Then a thought

came to her...an idea that might alleviate the tension between them and, at the same time, show Daniel how committed she was to this dinner.

"I've been thinking," she said. "Would you consider going on a date with me?"

His brows raised a fraction. "A date? Haven't we been out three nights this week?"

"I meant a few weeks down the road." She could see his confusion, so she hurried to explain. "I'd like for you to be my date for the dinner."

He said nothing.

"The fund-raising gala," she said as a gentle reminder.

"Sure."

"Listen..."

They spoke simultaneously, but Savanna heard the curtness in his too-swift acceptance.

"...if you'd rather not, it's okay. Really," she finished, giving him a chance to rescind.

"I'd like to go to the dinner with you," he said. "It's a date." He stuck out his hand to shake as though it were some kind of business deal they were sealing.

Savanna bit her bottom lip to keep from smiling

and looked down at his outstretched hand. "Do you think that's really necessary?"

He gave a self-conscious shrug and lowered his hand to his side.

She felt it would be prudent to change the subject to a more neutral topic.

"Have you had lunch?"

"Yes," he said. "But thanks for asking." Eyeing the white spatters on her arms, he commented, "You've been painting. I'm free the rest of the afternoon. Can I give you a hand?"

"Oh, no," she said, a frown firmly planted between her brows. "You'll ruin your suit..."

"No problem." As he spoke, he shrugged out of his jacket. "I'll just ditch the tie, roll up the shirtsleeves." His hands worked fast as he talked "And, voila! I'm ready to go to work."

"But your trousers. Your shoes," she complained. "I can't let you risk getting paint on your dress clothes."

"I want to," he insisted. "Upstairs?" He took her by the hand and tugged her toward the stairs.

As she trotted up the steps behind him, she felt her stomach churn with anticipation at spending time with the open and friendly Daniel who had returned as soon as the subject of the dinner was dropped. It was so obvious that he, too, was playing the ostrich, putting his distrust of her out of his head as much as possible. That fact told Savanna that Daniel liked spending time with her just as much as she liked spending time with him.

He started into the wrong room.

"No, no," she said. "Next door down."

Then Daniel stopped short.

"What have you done?"

Savanna nearly ran into his broad back. "What do you mean?" she asked.

Peering around him, she studied the room, the drop cloth covering the floor, the paintbrushes and roller she'd left out, the open bucket of paint. Then she saw what made him ask his question, made his tone a mixture of amusement and utter disbelief.

The walls were marred with long, irregular streaks of color. Some of the paint stripes were a bright white, while others were spread so thin that the beige undercoat clearly showed through.

"Who taught you how to paint?" Daniel asked, chuckling.

"No one," she said.

His mouth split into a wide grin. "Obviously."

"Hey," she said, her ego slightly injured. "I thought I was doing okay."

She walked to the center of the room and looked at the two walls she'd spent a good portion of the morning painting.

"Lord, what a mess," she muttered.

"It's all right." Daniel placed his hand on her shoulder. "We can fix it."

"You think so?" She twisted and looked into his face.

He nodded with confidence. "I'm certain of it."

The next thing she knew, she was painting with the roller and he was brandishing a paintbrush. But she hadn't made two swipes across the wall before Daniel stopped her.

"You can't cover the entire wall at one go. Try painting one small space at a time," he said. "Here, let me show you."

He stepped up behind her, reached around and curled his fingers over hers on the handle of the roller.

"Small strokes," he instructed, his voice a scant inch from her ear.

His breath tickled the sensitive flesh of her neck and a delicious shiver raced up her spine. He was so close, the intoxicating scent of his cologne overpowered the fresh paint smell that permeated the room. They stood, arm against arm, body against body, thigh against thigh, as he showed her the proper way to roll paint onto the wall.

"The reason you have so much streaking," he explained, "is because you were spreading the paint out too thin."

She barely heard his words; her attention focused on the feel of his hard chest against her back. The springy hairs of his bare forearm tickled her skin. His biceps muscles flexed against her shoulder with every upward swing of his arm. His tight stomach pressed to the small of her back; his taut thigh molding with hers.

Breathless and exuberant, she prayed he wouldn't move away from her too quickly. She enjoyed the closeness, and besides, she doubted her rubbery legs would hold her up on their own.

She blinked, realizing that they'd stopped pushing the roller. Instinctively she turned her head and found herself looking into Daniel's sexy, dark eyes.

He studied her a moment, and then commented softly, "We'll never get the room painted like this."

Savanna smiled at him.

Curling his index finger under her chin, he locked his gaze onto her lips.

"You don't know what that smile does to me," he murmured. He hovered there, his mouth a breath away from hers. Then he stepped away from her and picked up the paintbrush.

She refilled the roller with paint, more than a little disappointed that he turned out to be such a conscientious helper. And a blatant tease.

After a few minutes, Daniel said, "It's good to know that some things don't change." He pointed to the radio. "You still like soft pop."

A flush crept over her cheeks when she realized she was singing aloud. Badly.

"What can I say? I love love songs," she admitted. "Do you still like that stuff from the sixties?"

"Folk music," he said.

She chuckled. "Folk music, then."

His smile was lopsided as he said, "Give me a good croon from Bob Dylan any day,"

"But he's so...old."

"Oh, you wound me." He pressed his palm to his chest. Then his eyes twinkled as he grinned at her. "You were just doing a pretty good imitation of him, by the way. In his younger days, of course."

Turning back to face the wall, she feigned a huff and said, "I'll never sing to you again."

As she rolled the paint onto the wall, she was acutely aware of him. His every move demanded her attention. But he seemed totally concentrated on covering the wooden trim with white paint.

She couldn't help but wonder why being with him made her so gloriously happy. It wasn't just a physical thing. Even though she'd thoroughly enjoyed the kiss they had shared, even dreamed of enjoying another in the immediate future, the fact remained that they had shared only one kiss. The other times they'd had together over the past week had been spent in interesting and lively conversation, comfortable silence or good, old-fashioned teasing.

She liked Daniel and couldn't help but wonder if he felt the same about her. A dark cloud overshadowed her sunny thoughts. If he did feel the same as she, why hadn't he mentioned the fact that he was thinking of leaving? Why did he continue to distrust her?

There were some things she could do something

about, and some things she couldn't. Focusing on the pristine white wall, she put all her efforts into the job at hand.

An hour later, Savanna dropped the roller into the empty paint tray.

"How about a break?" she asked.

Daniel stood and stretched the kinks from his back. "Sounds good to me."

"I'll get us something to drink."

He caught her wrist as she passed him, and he turned her to face him.

In a husky voice, he said, "You look young in that getup. Really young."

She hitched up the neckline of her t-shirt from where it had slipped to reveal her bare shoulder. The self-conscious action forced her to look away from Daniel's serious gaze.

"Is that supposed to be a compliment?" The teasing quip belied the disquiet she felt.

"Oh," he was quick to add, "I know you're a full-grown woman underneath. I just thought you'd like to know you could still pass for an ornery teenager if you ever had the inclination to."

"Ornery teenager?"

The grin that played on his mouth held a

mixture of sensuousness and boyish charm, a combination Savanna found overwhelmingly alluring.

"And if I had the inclination?" The seductive sound of her voice surprised and pleased her both at the same time.

"Well," he said, his own tone tantalizingly sexy, "I thought, if you were ever in the mood for a little... fun."

As he said the last word, he reached up and smudged a glob of paint onto the tip of her nose.

"Hey!" Savanna swiped the back of her hand across the slick wetness. "You want to play, huh?"

She whirled around, grabbed the paint roller and wielded it like a weapon. Bending her legs, she lowered her center of gravity and balanced her weight first on one foot, then the other.

"You dirty rat," she imitated the gangsters from old-time movies. "I'm between you and the door, see. You'll never get out alive." She chuckled. "Or at least unpainted."

"Now wait a minute," he said. He straightened and took a step toward her. "I didn't mean to start anything."

"It's too late for regrets now, Mugsy."

Daniel laughed. "What? Have we been transported to some 1940s black and white gangster movie?" He took another step forward. "Come on," he coaxed. "Give me the roller."

He stretched out his hand and Savanna saw a perfect opportunity, an opportunity of which she intended to take full advantage.

With the speed of a jackrabbit, she pushed the roller up the length of his flattened palm.

"I can't believe you did that!"

Daniel crouched like a defensive linebacker and Savanna shrieked. She dodged past him, but he caught her around the waist. They tumbled to the floor, a laughing, squealing, paint-flinging mess.

"You shouldn't have done that, Copper." Now he, too, mimicked hackneyed films of yesteryear.

She struggled under his weight. The hint of threat in his words may have been made teasingly, but she knew he meant to retaliate.

"Take this, you dirty rat."

Savanna felt his paint-streaked hand span her thigh and, for an instant, a jolt of desire shot through her. But then his fingers trailed down her leg, leaving behind a wet, sticky streak of paint. She screeched and laughed at the same time.

They sat up both breathing hard from their escapade. She saw him look at her and a fresh bout of chuckling had him holding his stomach.

"What's so funny?"

"I think," he commented, pulling out his handkerchief, "that you came out of this a little more painted than you intended."

He gently wiped her jaw, and she realized that she must have pressed her cheek against the paint roller during the tussle.

Daniel stood and then held out his hand to help her up.

"Truce?" he asked.

Savanna grinned up at him. "Truce."

"Go get yourself a shower," he said. "I'll wash up at the kitchen sink."

"I'll hurry," she called over her shoulder.

As she came down the stairs, showered, dressed and paint-free, Savanna heard the strains of a tinkling Mother Goose tune floating in from outside. She ran down the last few steps and over to the screen door.

"It's the ice cream man. The ice cream man!"

Running out onto the porch, she searched the street.

"You want a cone?"

She turned to see Daniel sitting on the porch, two glasses of iced tea on the small table beside the rocking chair.

"I'd love one," she said gleefully. "I used to get an ice cream treat almost every day when I was a kid."

The excitement twinkling in her eyes and her wide smile took Daniel's breath away. God, he loved just looking at her. Her carefree exuberance was downright irresistible.

"Wait right here," he told her.

He jogged to the curb and flagged down the truck.

"Two vanilla cones, please." He fished some dollar bills from his pocket. "Oh," he added, "dip one of those in chocolate sprinkles."

On his way toward the house, he studied Savanna as she sat on the step waiting for him. Her whole body conveyed the anticipation she felt. Daniel could feel it himself. He'd enjoyed getting to know her again over the past week.

A small frown wrinkled his brow as a tiny voice in his head asked, What will you do when you wake up one morning and find that she's abandoned you, and the hospital, and all the people of Fulton?

He knew it was going to happen. Just as sure as the sun would rise, he was certain that Savanna would someday leave him and the people at the hospital high and dry. Well, he might not *know* it, but he'd be a fool if he didn't remain vigilant of the possibility.

"Damn it," he muttered under his breath, willing the dark thoughts to the back of his brain. Maybe he wouldn't even be around to deal with the mess she was sure to cause. Maybe. But if he was still in Fulton when she disappointed the townspeople, he'd deal with it. He had once, he could do it again. But for the moment, he wanted to enjoy the simple pleasure of just being with her.

"Here you go." He handed her the cone covered in chocolate sprinkles and then sat on the porch step next to her. "And by the way, it was an ice cream woman."

He watched her tongue flick out to capture some of the chocolate candies coating the ice cream.

"Mmmm."

Tension knotted in his stomach, hot and tight. He wanted her, he couldn't deny it. But his instinct for self-preservation saved him. Kept him from rubbing his thumb over her ice-cream-coated lips. Kept him from tasting the chocolate sprinkles that were melting on her tongue.

"You know," she commented, "Fulton is such a beautiful place. The people are true neighbors. They care about each other. You don't find that much where I live. Don't get me wrong, I've made some good friends. But it's just not the same."

Daniel licked at a drip of ice cream that was sliding down his sugar cone.

"I've never seen an ice cream truck traveling down the street I live on." Savanna wiped at the corners of her mouth with her fingers. "If someone from Fulton had a problem and needed to call the police, chances are he'd know the policeman, feel comfortable that someone was concerned." She grimaced. "In the city, you're lucky to have the police show up. And they're so hardened by the things they experienced, they don't have it in them to feel excessive concern. Maintaining the law is just another job in the city."

What she said was most probably true, Daniel mused.

"Towns like Fulton take care of their own,"

Savanna went on. "I remember the Christmas before I left there was a family whose house burned down. Mom and I took them blankets and clothes."

From the faraway look in Savanna's eyes, Daniel could tell she was caught up in a memory.

"That family told us about the help they'd received. Not just household items, but money and groceries, even toys and gifts for the children's Christmas." She nodded, her eyes still distant. "Fulton takes care of its own...where, in the city, there's so much coming and going, it's hard to even get to know who's living next door to you."

Daniel took a bite of his cone. Fulton was a good town, a wholesome town. Everything Savanna said was true. He could easily recall people who had been helped and cared for when they were unable to do for themselves. Hadn't friends and neighbors showed his family kindness and caring when his father had died? And Fulton had other quaint qualities.

Only in a small town would you find the school buses dropping children off right at their front doors, or mailmen who stopped in for coffee and a discussion of local affairs. Or ice cream trucks offering frozen confections that had children screaming with delight.

Fulton was a town he wanted to live in. Daniel sat up straight, realizing in that instant that he'd made an important decision.

He looked at the woman beside him. It had taken Savanna, someone who had left Fulton and returned to notice all that she had been missing, to make him see that he never wanted to leave.

"Listen," he said, popping the last bit of cone into his mouth. "I have to run. There's something I need to do."

"But, your jacket..."

"I'll get it later," he promised, then strode off with purpose in his step.

* * *

Humidity weighed down the hot air. Thin cirrus clouds scudded high across the night sky, casting lacy shadows on the lawn. The quiet was heavenly. The temperature inside the air-conditioned house would have been a whole lot more comfortable. Still Savanna continued to sit on the porch swing, sipping at her half-empty glass of merlot.

After Daniel had left in such a hurry this afternoon, she'd cleaned up the paint mess and then she'd pulled out the file she'd been compiling on the gala dinner. The few phone contacts she'd intended to make had turned into nearly two dozen calls made and received, and by the time she'd finished for the day, her ear actually hurt and her neck had been stiff from holding the phone in the crook of her shoulder as she'd talked, shuffled papers and taken notes.

Her mind had continued to whirr with thoughts about the fund-raising event as she'd eaten a little dinner and then slipped into the shower. She should have gone to bed hours ago, but organizing these events energized her to the point that sleep was often elusive.

Sitting here enjoying the night, absorbing the calm, was just what she needed.

A pair of headlights caught her attention and she watched as a car moved along the street, slowing as it neared her house. She recognized Daniel's car even before it had a chance to come to a full stop. He sat behind the steering wheel for nearly a full minute, the engine continuing to purr.

She stood and took the few steps that brought her out of the shadows so he could see her.

Moonlight struck the satin of her short kimono-type robe and lit the white fabric like a beacon.

The car's engine went silent, and then Daniel opened the driver's side door and got out. He paused a moment before heading toward her.

When he was close enough, she softly asked, "Are you okay? It's got to be after midnight."

He tilted his head a fraction and placed his hand on the post at the base of the porch stairs. "I'm here to pick up my jacket."

A quiet chuckle bubbled from her. "That sounds more like a question than an answer."

She realized he was staring at her bare feet, and she instinctively crossed one over the other.

"You should be wearing slippers," he told her. "Or socks. Or something."

Savanna smiled. "What? You don't like the color of my polish?"

He returned her grin. "You could get a splinter from those floor boards."

They both spoke in hushed tones. There was something almost reverent about the still, hot silence of the night.

"I'll be okay." She leaned her shoulder against

the column. "But I'm not at all sure about you. What brings you out so late?"

Daniel lifted one shoulder. "I wanted to see you. Talk to you. I didn't want to call and risk waking you, and I wasn't going to ring the bell if I didn't see any lights on.'

When he didn't elaborate further, she pushed. "But... are you all right?"

"Yes," he said. "I'm better than all right, actually."

But, again, he fell silent rather than expand on his thoughts, and his expression remained stoic. He slid his hands into the pockets of his dress trousers and lightly jangled his car keys.

Savanna lifted her wine glass. "Would you like something to drink? I've got merlot. And I think Dad left some scotch in his study."

A small smile played at the corners of his mouth. "A scotch would be great, thanks."

She turned and went inside, and he came up the step, following her through the front door, the open foyer and into the study. Savanna flipped on a small lamp and went to the liquor cabinet. She inspected the highball glass before up-righting it onto the cabinet top, and then she pulled out a decanter of scotch.

"Ice?" she asked, realizing that would necessitate a trip to the kitchen.

He shook his head. "Neat is fine."

She poured a jigger of the amber liquid, capped the crystal decanter and handed the glass to Daniel.

"Thanks." He looked down into the glass, but didn't take a drink. "I have to tell you, this feels weird."

As he spoke, she'd taken a sip of wine. Once she swallowed, she asked, "Weird?"

"Yes. You know." He lifted the scotch. "Drinking in your father's house."

She laughed. "We're all grown up now, Daniel. I promise you, Dad would not disapprove of my offering you a cocktail."

He sighed and arched his brows. "If you say so. But I don't mind telling you, being in this house makes me feel..." he paused a moment, "...like a randy teenager again." He took a gulp of the scotch.

"Believe me," she told him, "I know exactly what you mean."

What she'd meant to convey was that being in her childhood home often made her feel more the adolescent than the adult, but when her gaze clashed with Daniel's she realized that he'd completely misconstrued what she'd said.

Suddenly, she felt as though someone has sucked all the air out of the room, and she felt the need to drag a lungful of oxygen into her body. His dark eyes focused directly onto hers and the quiet clanged as jarring as cymbals.

Say something, dammit. The voice in her head screamed at her, but she was caught fast in this startling and silken trap that had seemingly struck her dumb.

"Can we sit?" he asked.

"Of course." She moved to the sofa.

The aged leather was worn and felt supple against her bare calves when she sat and tucked her feet up on the cushion beneath her. Daniel eased himself down much closer than she expected. She could feel the warmth of him, the solid mass of him.

Savanna sensed he wanted to talk, but as the seconds ticked by, she became a little nervous.

Tension continued to build until she could no longer stand it.

She blurted, "Remember when we snuck into the liquor cabinet?"

The memory made him shake his head. "Don't remind me."

Laughter rumbled from deep in her chest. She pressed her fingers to her lips in an attempt to stifle it, but it slipped out nonetheless. "I'm sorry. That was all my fault. I never should have suggested it."

He shrugged. "I deserved the stern talking to your dad gave me. I was older. I should have known better."

"Mom must have marked the bottle. It was only wine, for gosh sakes." Her shoulders shook with mirth. "And we only had a little. The way they acted, you'd think we were falling down drunk."

She watched him take another sip from his glass as she said, "I got you into all sorts of trouble, didn't I?"

His chuckle was low, and he shifted on the couch, resting his arm along the back. His fingertips were a breath away from her shoulder.

"It's okay," he told her. "I didn't mind. I actually enjoyed myself. Most of the time."

A strand of her hair had fallen across her chest and she reached up and absently smoothed the lock between her index finger and thumb. "Still, I'm sorry I got you into so much hot water back then." Then her grin widened. "But I have to say, it sure was easy to talk you into my schemes."

He paused long enough to take a deep breath. "Savanna," he said softly, "you had a way of looking at me that made me feel..." he searched for the right word "...invincible. When I was with you, I became the 'go to' guy. The person who could make things happen. You made me feel smarter than everyone else, more capable. You made me feel proud of myself." His tone grew more serious as he continued, "With you, I felt stronger... faster... more..." He seemed at a loss.

"Better?" she offered teasingly.

He laughed suddenly. "That's it. More better. More better than everyone else."

She tucked her bottom lip between her teeth. Oh, if he only knew how she'd felt about him then. In her opinion, he *had* been the most intelligent man she'd ever known, and the most capable, the strongest, the very best in every way, not to mention the absolute sexiest. He had been everything she'd ever wanted. Everything she'd ever needed. But making that admission, admitting just how crazy in love with him she had been, would make her too vulnerable for comfort. So instead, she whispered, "That's exactly what you were, Daniel." Her throat constricted and her next two words came out sounding strained. "More better."

Tears threatened to well up in her eyes, and Savanna lifted her wine glass to her lips to give her a few seconds to get herself together.

"Remember when we went to that slasher movie?"

Daniel's question opened the floodgates of her memories and she grinned. "Mom forbid me to see that film!"

"Which you failed to tell me until *after* I'd bought the tickets."

"I know." Savanna wrinkled her nose. "I was bad. But all my friends were talking about that movie. They'd all seen it. I felt so left out."

"We might have gotten away with it had you not left the ticket stub in your jacket pocket."

"I know." She performed another nose crinkle.

"But that was your fault. Love short-circuited my brain."

The 'L word' had slipped off her tongue before she'd had time to stop it, but he continued as if he hadn't even heard it.

"Your mother was furious with me. With both of us." Then he chuckled as he added, "Do you know how hard it was for me not to tell her that neither one of us saw much of the movie?"

The question caused a languorous smile to spread across her mouth, then their eyes met and held, both of them remembering the smoldering kisses they'd shared in the shadows, tucked away in the very back row. It all seemed so excruciatingly innocent now; he, just starting college, she still in high school, dealing with curfews and restrictions, stealing passionate kisses in the dark confines of a movie theater.

Savanna had always been aware of how lucky she'd been that he'd been attracted to her. He could have dated girls his own age; girls who, being more mature, would have been freer to go and see and do more of the things that interested a young man. But Daniel had seemed content, happy even, to spend his time with her. And they'd spent every available moment together.

"If your parents knew about even half the stuff we did, they'd have locked you in your room until after you'd graduated high school." He shook his head.

Their antics had been harmless, of course. But some of the day trips they'd gone on stood out in her memory. He'd taken her to the botanical gardens in Richmond. Daniel had brought along his camera, and he'd made her feel beautiful the way he'd continued snapping photos of her among the flowers. He'd taken her shopping in Roanoke; the little hole-in-the-wall restaurant where they'd lunched had served surprisingly good food along with an incomparable romantic ambiance. And some of her fondest memories had been when they'd slipped away to Virginia Beach. Golden sunshine, warm sand, gentle surf, and the feel of his hands on her body as he'd applied sunscreen lotion to her skin. If she closed her eyes, she could easily imagine gliding her fingers over the hard hills and valleys of his muscles as she'd smoothed warm lotion on his back and shoulders.

"Why is everything more fun when it's off-limits?"

Her eyelids fluttered open at the sound of his voice. She hadn't realized how lost she'd become in the past. Looking into his handsome face now, she realized just how much fun they'd had, how many places they had experienced together. All that time spent laughing, all those endless hours of talking and planning and dreaming had allowed them to come to know each other so well.

Too well.

That low, throaty tone, the intensity in those luscious eyes, the way the muscles on either side of his mouth tensed just the slightest bit. Seduction laced that question like a fancy French garter.

His gaze broke from hers, roving over her face and then traveling down her torso like a physical touch.

"Why *is* that?" he murmured. "What makes forbidden fruit taste so sweet?" He traced the curve of her bare shoulder with the pad of his thumb. Then his breath left him in a ragged exhalation. "You're beautiful, Savanna."

She reached up and slid her fingers over the facings of her delicate robe. "Well," she croaked,

"I wore such hideous pj's as a kid...stiff cotton...flannel..." she chuckled nervously "...I splurge these days."

Without taking his eyes off her body, he leaned forward long enough to set the highball glass on the coffee table. "I'm not talking about what you're wearing."

Something in her brain blocked out the compliment and she rambled on, "I love the feel of silk and satin. Makes me feel... pretty."

The small, lazy circles he drew on her shoulder felt delicious and sent heat coursing through her.

"But you looked pretty in flannel."

As he uttered that final word, a spark lit his gaze and his mouth contracted into half-smile. All Savanna wanted to do was reach out and glide her fingertips over his jaw, over those luscious lips. But then she blinked.

You looked pretty in flannel.

In a flash, she was captured by some strange mental time warp and flung back to *that* night... *that* moment... when they'd made love for the very first time.

She'd been so young when they'd first started dating that Daniel had insisted that the physical intimacies they shared didn't go too far. Even months later, after they had professed their love for one another and Savanna felt 'ready'... ready to go further... ready to prove her love by giving him all she had to give, he was determined that they wait.

They both suffered months of needless frustration, she'd felt. He already owned her heart. He was already in nearly every waking thought she had. Why shouldn't they express themselves in what she'd always believed was the purest form of love? It was implied in every Jane Austen novel she'd ever read, was blatantly depicted in every romantic movie she'd ever seen. Sex was the most normal and natural declaration of the heart. Besides that, the hormones raging through her body were enough to drive her completely insane. Savanna needed some sort of release.

When she had pushed him, he'd been adamant that they would wait until her eighteenth birthday, and although she had thought it was a sweet gesture on his part, she was just as adamant that they would not. She began saying and doing everything she could think of to force him to surrender to her wiles. Oh, what a spicy, seductive battle it had been.

Never would she have guessed that his breaking point would be seeing her in a pair of flannel boxer shorts.

She tilted her head to the side, brushing at the lock of hair that tickled her upper arm. "What happened to you that night?" The question came out in a feathery whisper.

Silence swelled and stretched between them until she could hear her heart thudding, and with each passing second the desire he felt for her grew. She saw it in his eyes, sensed it in every tense muscle of his body. His throat convulsed as he swallowed. And she realized that she wanted him just as much as he wanted her.

Finally, he moistened his lips and answered, "I don't know." Then he immediately shook his head. "No. That's not true. Not true at all."

He slipped the wine glass from her hand and set it on the coffee table, and once he leaned back on the sofa, he reached out and picked up one end of the sash of her robe.

"I'd been away at college," he began, studying the sash as if the satin held some great secret. "I hadn't seen you for weeks."

The letters she'd written him had been filled with her angst.

"It had been almost impossible to focus on my classes. I was surrounded by my friends, my classmates and my professors, but I don't think I've ever felt so lonely in my life. I didn't think the semester would ever end."

She'd suffered the same distraction and desolation.

"I was expecting you Friday night," she told him. "But you surprised me."

His left shoulder lifted then fell. "I finished exams a day early. Packing up and driving home just seemed like the thing to do."

Savanna's heart constricted. "You threw pebbles at my bedroom window."

"I couldn't wait until morning to see you."

A knot of emotion rose in her throat and she swallowed in an attempt to allay it.

He'd missed her. Wanted her. That came as no surprise. He'd loved her. She'd loved him. Desperately. But the sheer magnitude of what they'd felt for each other struck her in a poignant and powerful way.

She curled her fingers and tucked her hand

beneath her chin. "This might sound corny as hell, but I felt like Juliet that night, opening the window to my Romeo."

"Oh, yeah." He snickered. "That's corny as hell."

"Daniel!" She gave his arm a light slap, but she couldn't help laughing too.

His smile lingered as he admitted, "At least you've been able to put a positive spin on it."

Her jaw went slack. "You don't think of that night as something good?"

"No, no, it's not that." His brow tensed. "It's just that I was conflicted. I still am. I couldn't help feeling that what we were doing was so wrong." He went very still. "Let's face it, what I'm saying is true. You were still seventeen."

"My birthday was just a few weeks away." Her point was all but lost in the sulky tone of her voice and the childishly stubborn lift of her chin.

"Savanna, we made love right here." He touched the couch cushion with his index finger. "We had unprotected sex in your father's study." He arched his brows as he added, "And your parents were asleep upstairs."

She pressed her lips together, unable to deny the truth of what he said. They had both fretted for days and days afterward, until she'd cycled and they realized that they were safe.

Daniel closed his eyes then, emitting the tiniest of groans. "But there were things about that night that were *so* right."

He captured her hand in his and looked into her eyes. He gently pulled open her fingers. The kiss he placed on the center of her palm was deliciously soft, but the addition of a small, hot lick shifted everything. Her blood pulsed thickly through her veins. And when his dark gaze met hers again, she knew without a doubt where this was headed.

"We probably shouldn't," he grated.

"You're probably right."

Savanna ran her tongue over her lips, pondering. She wasn't a teenager any longer. And if there was one thing she'd learned since leaving Fulton all those years ago, it was that calm, rational thinking was the best way to make decisions.

To hell with that, she thought, pulling her hand from his and sliding her bottom onto his lap. The feel of his day-old beard against her fingertips was utterly tantalizing.

Doubt sparked in his eyes and he said her name, but she silenced him with a kiss.

"You want this," she whispered against his mouth. "I want this."

Bare hunger shoved aside any hint of misgiving he might have been feeling. His hand skimmed along her thigh, skittered beneath the hem of her robe. His touch was scorching hot and softer than the satin she fully intended to shrug out of. The lacy elastic of her panties was no hindrance as his fingers slid beneath it to trace the curve of her hip.

He said her name again, but this time his low, ragged timbre expressed every ounce of the desire rushing through him.

Her need for him pulsed, hot and wet.

"Shut up, Daniel," she said. "Just shut up and make love to me."

CHAPTER NINE

———

"Can I give you a hand?" Savanna asked.

"Sure." Sheila motioned for Savanna to sit beside her on the back step. "Snapping beans is probably my least favorite chore."

Picking up a long, firm green bean, Savanna snapped off both ends. "I haven't done this since I was a little girl." She tossed the bean into the bowl at Sheila's feet and reached into the bag for another.

"I can remember the smell that permeated the whole house when Mom cooked up a pot of beans and potatoes. She'd add some smoked ham."

Savanna rolled her eyes and smacked her lips at the memory. "It tasted as wonderful as it smelled."

Both women fell silent, the sound of snapping hovering in the hot afternoon air.

"Where are the kids?" Savanna asked.

"I hired the Stevensons' daughter to take them to the park." Sheila smiled wearily. "Patty's nearly eighteen. And she's really good with Amanda. Keeps an eagle eye on my little urchin."

"You look tired," Savanna said. "You should be taking a nap instead of out here in the sun doing chores."

Sheila shrugged. "It's got to get done. Besides, I'm okay." She shot Savanna a lopsided grin. "Haven't you heard? Being tired is synonymous with being pregnant."

"Still," Savanna said, refusing to back down until her concern was voiced, "you should take care of yourself."

"I do," Sheila said. "Don't you worry." She gathered another handful of beans. "Jim says plans for the dinner are going well."

She nodded. "It's almost scary. Businesses are calling me to offer their help. I've never had anything like this happen before. People from all over the county are calling. This fund-raising dinner has been smooth sailing from the very beginning."

Sheila lowered her head, intent on her bean snapping. In a low voice she commented, "Looks like your relationship with Daniel has been smooth sailing too."

Savanna chuckled and gave Sheila's knee a light nudge. "Hey, you don't have to hedge. I don't mind telling you about what's happening between me and Daniel."

"Well..." Sheila raised one shoulder. "I don't want to seem nosy."

"You're my friend," Savanna told her. "You could never be nosy."

At that, Sheila surrendered to her curiosity, sliding an inch closer. "So tell me."

"Things are...great."

Sheila's hands stopped and lowered into her lap. "Why the hesitation?" She studied Savanna with concern. "From the tone of your voice it sounds as though you don't think things between you and Daniel should be great."

"It's not that." Then she sighed. "I came back to

Fulton to straighten out everything. To explain to him what happened six years ago."

"And you did that. Right?"

"I think so." The three small words harbored a boatload of doubt. "And, like I said, things between us are good. But I just don't understand myself." She twirled the green bean between her fingers without really seeing it. "I don't understand what it is I'm feeling."

"Tell me. Maybe I can help."

Savanna snapped the stem off the bean. "I really enjoy being with Daniel."

"There's some law against that?"

Smiling, Savanna said, "Of course not. I'm happy that we're getting along so well. It's just that I never expected to...feel so..." The rest of the sentence withered as she searched for words to express herself. Inhaling deeply, she started again. "He just makes me too happy."

Sheila's brows drew together. "*Too* happy? I've never heard of such a thing."

"Sheila, I feel all giddy inside when I'm with him. I find myself worrying about what I'm wearing, how I look. When we're together, I'm afraid I'm going to say something wrong, something to embarrass myself. I'm just, I don't know, on edge all the time. In a good way, of course. And when he kisses me..."

"He kisses you?" Sheila's eyes were wide.

Savanna nodded. "Yeah. He has," she said, her voice taking on a dreamy quality. "And when he touches me..."

"*What?* You two got down and dirty, and you didn't tell me?"

"I'm telling you now."

Sheila snapped the bean she held in her fingers, tossed it in with the others, then set the bowl aside. "I don't mean to be nosey or anything, but was it, you know, good?"

The mere memory of that night still made her breathless. "Sheila, it was better than good." *More better*, she thought grinning to herself. "Daniel came over and we started talking about the past. We just got caught up in memories; that was all it was. But it was... earth-shattering." The image of him untying the sash of her robe and slipping it off her shoulders made her shiver, even now. "We shouldn't have, of course. Daniel even said so. And I knew he was right. But you know how bull-headed I can be."

From the thunderstruck look on her face, Sheila could have been knocked over by a single light touch to the forehead.

"It didn't *mean* anything," Savanna stressed, unable to look into Sheila's eyes any longer as she repeated, "Of course, it didn't mean anything. It was just a lovely romp, is all. Consensual sex between two adults who..." she scrambled for words "...have a history together. It meant nothing."

She took a deep breath and gazed out into the yard. "But I can't stop thinking about it. I can't stop thinking about *him*. I mean... the way he looked at me. The way he kissed me. Touched me." She swallowed. "And the way he smiled afterward. I want to see that again. I want to feel that... again. I just... I want... more. Of *that*. Of him. Of... something."

Suddenly filled with frustration, Savanna threw the green bean into the bowl. "See there? I'm babbling like a fool."

"You're talking like you're in love." Sheila's comment was barely above a whisper.

Savanna cast her a sidelong glance. "You've got

to be kidding. There's no way I'm in love with Daniel. I didn't come back to Fulton for that."

"Maybe you didn't," Sheila said, "but let's look at this logically. Daniel makes you happy. He makes you giddy. He makes you worry. He makes you afraid. He makes you edgy—in a good way, of course," she teased, counting off on her fingers. "And when he kisses you..."

"It's wonderful," Savanna finished the sentence, closing her eyes and drawing it out to a lazy and languorous end.

"Not to mention," Sheila said, enunciating as if she were speaking to a dimwit, "you slept together."

"Now, wait," she protested. "I told you. That..."

"Yeah, yeah, yeah. It meant nothing." Sheila snatched up the bowl and began snapping beans again. "But you want more. More of *that*. More of Daniel." She paused, her brows arching high. "Okay, so what's with the stink eye? Don't be mad at me. I'm just repeating your words." Then she shook her head. "Girl, you not only got it, you got it bad."

Savanna's shoulders drooped, and then she opened her mouth to speak but closed it, and then repeated the action in a perfect imitation of a fish out of water. Finally, her gaze connected with Sheila's as she realized aloud, "I'm in love with Daniel. How on earth did *that* happen?"

"Maybe," her friend murmured, "you never stopped.

* * *

The fund-raiser meeting seemed interminable. The board members were taking turns going over various details of the dinner. Their proclivity of looking at things up-ways, down-ways and inside-out would help to assure success in the end; however, this kind of micro-managing took *hours*.

She found herself stealing a glance across the conference table at Daniel. He'd barely greeted her when he'd arrived. Granted, he'd come into the room just as the meeting was starting, but would it hurt him to smile at her?

Savanna had never in her wildest imaginings thought she'd fall in love with the very man she'd run away from six years earlier. Questions rolled through her head like a fast-moving silent film.

What should she do now? Profess her feelings? Or wait for some sign from him? Savanna leaned against the chair back, darting a quick look at him.

His mouth was pulled into a surly line. Oh, gosh, was he regretting having come to her house? Was he sorry they'd made love? He had expressed doubt that night. Hell, she silently lamented, why hadn't she listened to him?

"On the other hand, he certainly hadn't put up much of a fight. If he hadn't wanted-"

"Savanna?"

Jim Thompson's voice snapped her to attention. She blinked. "Yes? Sorry. Must have checked out there for a moment."

"I asked how many tickets have been sold. For the dinner."

"Eighty-five percent," she stated, thankful at her quick recovery. "And there's still two weeks to go. I'm sure we'll sell them all."

Savanna hesitated a moment until the murmurs of excitement subsided.

"I sold four tickets to the mayor." Miz Ida's shoulders squared proudly. "Will we have any other distinguished guests?"

"We have quite a few mayors from the surrounding towns," Savanna told her, "and at least one senator. One former governor. Several of Virginia's most prominent authors will be there.

I've got a model, two actors, a former Miss America, and a NASCAR driver. I'm working on a second. All of these people were born and raised in Virginia." She started naming names and heard happy murmurings around the table. "Oh, and I don't think I mentioned it before," she continued, "but I was contacted by two musical groups, offering to entertain for free. I accepted both offers."

"How is that going to work?" Daniel's curt question cut her off.

She glanced over at him, startled by the harshness of his tone. "Well..."

"What died and crawled up your butt, Daniel?" Miz Ida asked none too gently.

Savanna appreciated the support.

Then Jim said, "Ida, I think it's a legitimate question."

She cleared her throat. "As I was saying, I accepted both. The Bradley Brothers play jazz and will entertain as dinner is served, and the set will last through the dessert course. Then after a slight intermission, about nine, Times Gone By will take over. I don't know if any of you have heard of them, but they specialize in the big-band sound. They've put out several CDs. They've agreed to play until midnight."

"Oh," one woman piped up, "they are *fabulous*." She was sitting right beside Daniel and she addressed him as she added, "They played at my sister's wedding. Abigail was getting married for the fourth time, you know, and that band was just *fabulous*." Each time she stressed the word "fabulous," she tapped Daniel on the forearm. "I danced till dawn." The woman's eyes glittered. "It was just *fabulous*." Again she tapped.

Savanna pressed her lips together, reining in an unexpected grin, as she watched Daniel grit his teeth.

He turned toward her with a gaze so sharp she expected to be cut in half.

"Did you clear this with the manager of the country club?"

The urge to smile disappeared completely. "Of course I did," she snapped.

"Of course she did," Miz Ida parroted.

But Daniel continued to press. "Do you have a contract with these bands?"

"Well, no," she admitted. "They're playing for free."

He frowned. "What if they decide not to show up?"

The question felt like a personal attack. "Why would they do that?"

"Oh, I don't know," he said breezily. "They're offered a paying gig at the last minute?"

"But both bands know how important this is," she said. "They called me. They offered to play to help the hospital."

"If they don't show up," Miz Ida proclaimed boldly, "then we have the dinner with no music. Doesn't seem like the end of the world to me."

The woman sitting beside Daniel screeched, "What kind of party would that be?"

Savanna focused on her notes and thought it best to change the subject entirely. "Oh, yes," she said. "Charlie Hickman of Hickman Travel Agency here in Fulton called me. He's donating a trip for two to the Bahamas."

"My word!" Ida said. "I can't believe it. Charlie Hickman is so tight his shoes squeak when he walks. He donated a trip?"

"Yes," Savanna happily confirmed. "The package includes airfare and five nights' accommodation in a four-star hotel right on the beach."

"That's just *fabulous*," the woman next to Daniel said, tapping him on the arm.

"And just what," Daniel intoned flatly, "are you going to do with a trip for two to the Bahamas?"

It wasn't the question that sparked a fiery anger in Savanna. The inquiry was perfectly reasonable. What infuriated her beyond words was the tone in which the question had been asked.

Granted, he doubted her ability to successfully pull off these events. At each and every meeting he had probed and questioned, forcing her to prove that she was dotting every i and crossing every t. But tonight's verbal assault was especially critical.

She pressed her lips firmly together and inhaled deeply. This didn't have anything to do with bands or contracts or trips. This had to do with one thing, and one thing only. Sex. Daniel regretted having slept with her. And he was expressing that by attacking her.

Savanna felt her back teeth clench. Maybe she'd been a bit pushy that night. But she refused to accept all the blame. He was a big boy. He could have stopped everything with a simple no.

Time and again she'd made allowances for him at these meetings because she knew he distrusted her, she knew he expected her to run off and leave Fulton before the fund-raising dinner plans were complete. She'd even sympathized with him, knowing what she'd done to him six years ago. She'd hoped to make him realize, by her hard work and dedication, that she could be trusted. But it was so obvious to her that he would never learn to trust her. No matter how much time and effort, planning and devotion she gave to the people of Fulton, Daniel would never see she was worthy of his confidence. The realization knifed through her, slashing to the very depth of her soul. Hurting her as much, if not more, than knowing he regretted having sex with her.

She sat in that room filled with people she'd worked with, people she'd come to know again, people she'd come to love, and she clearly understood she had two choices. She could give in to the pain she felt, give in to the tears of frustration and insult that threatened to spill. Or she could stoke up a blazing ire and send it coursing through every muscle in her body.

It took a nanosecond for anger to win.

Swallowing the lump that had risen in her throat, she fixed Daniel with a burning glare. "Well, Mr. Walsh," she addressed him, her voice ominously low. "To tell you the truth, I haven't decided what I'm going to do with the trip yet. I may use it as a door prize, or I may auction off this amazing tropical excursion to the highest bidder. Let's not forget that making money for the hospital is our goal here. Right?"

She stood, the chair tottering on its two back legs for a split second before coming to rest on all fours again. Resentment burned in her like a white-hot incandescent flame.

"Everyone in this room knows how you detested the idea of my helping out in these fund-raising projects," she said. "Everyone has heard you question me at every turn. Everyone knows you expect me to *run away*." She put ugly emphasis on the two words "Everyone knows exactly what you think of me."

Her jaw tightened as fury blazed through every pore of her body, singed every cell. Planting her splayed hands on the table, she leaned her weight on them and hurled her hostility at the man who denied her the one simple thing that had come to mean nearly everything to her. His trust.

"I don't know why you're so concerned, anyway," she replied in a shaky, barely controlled voice. "What with that prestigious partnership offer you're considering with that mega-money law firm in Richmond, why, you're the one who won't be here for the dinner. Not me. You're the one who's running out on everyone. Not me!"

The room was utterly silent. It seemed that no one even breathed as they waited to hear Daniel's response.

Animosity flickered in his harsh gaze. He stood with slow deliberateness. His spine was straight, his shoulders high and square, as he quietly said, "With Savanna Langford back in Fulton, who could blame me for hightailing it out of town?"

He couldn't have stunned her more had he physically smacked her.

Then he walked out of the conference room.

"Oh, Savanna."

Miz Ida's disapproving voice pierced through the thick fog that enveloped Savanna's brain.

"I didn't know Daniel was thinking of leaving us," someone whispered.

"What law firm was she talking about?"

"I did hear something about that."

"Will somebody please tell me what's going on?"

Everyone talked at once and the meeting fell into complete and utter chaos.

Savanna's knees gave way and she sank back into her chair. The anger drained from her as though someone pulled the plug out of a water-filled tub.

The rumor had been that he was thinking of leaving town because of her, but she hadn't wanted to believe it. But now she knew it was true. She'd heard him say it. He was leaving because of her. *Because of her.*

She felt hollow and empty. Her throat burned with the acid left behind by the hurtful words she'd flung at him.

If Daniel moves away, Ida's words echoed through Savanna's mind, *the people of Fulton will be losing someone special.*

Fulton will be losing someone special.

Someone special.

Dear Lord, what had she done? She couldn't let this happen. This was all her fault. She'd slid her satin-clad butt on his lap. She'd told him to shut up and kiss her. She'd practically demanded that he make love to her. What kind of way was *that* to garner the man's trust?

She had to fix this. She had to find him. Had to talk to him. And make him change his mind.

Savanna murmured a vague apology to everyone murmuring around the conference table and then headed out of the room, without thought for her purse, briefcase or notes.

"Savanna, wait," Jim Thompson called.

But she was out the door, her feet fairly flying down the tiled hallway. She slid half a foot as she made the first sharp turn that would take her to the hospital's main entrance. As she turned the next corner, she collided with a white-uniformed orderly.

"My fault," she said, waving off his apologies. "Did you see Mr. Walsh? Daniel Walsh?"

"Yes," the surprised young man said. "He's waiting for the elevator."

"Thanks," she called over her shoulder.

The elevator doors were just gliding shut as she reached them. Savanna cursed under her breath and turned toward the door leading to the stairs.

Her heart felt as though it would burst as she

rushed down the steps, two at a time. Bursting onto the first floor, she ran toward the front entrance.

She was impervious to the hot, muggy air that hit her full-force in the face as she erupted into the night.

"Daniel!" she called.

He was in the parking lot, his back to her. He didn't stop.

"Daniel, please," she shouted, continuing to run toward him. "Wait!"

The high-powered street lamp threw shadows over his face when he turned to face her. Her chest was heaving, her lungs burning, when she stopped a few feet from him.

"Please," she said, panting. "I need to talk to you."

"Seems to me you've already said plenty."

"I know. And I'm sorry. I shouldn't have said any of that. I shouldn't have told everyone your plans."

"My plans?" He gave a derisive laugh. "And just how the hell did you find out about my plans, anyway?"

Savanna tucked her bottom lip between her teeth. Finally she gave a little shrug, refusing to add to her sins by incriminating Ida.

Daniel shook his head. "The rumors fly fast and furious in this town, don't they? I guess I already knew that..." He sighed and dragged his fingers through his hair.

She gave a small nod of her head.

"I know," she said, her voice sounding weak to her ears, "there were rumors floating around about me too. Rumors that said I had plans of staying on in Fulton."

He moved to speak, but she cut him off with one upraised palm. She had to do this. She might not want to, but she had to.

"Let me finish." She swallowed and gathered the courage to tell him the truth. "Daniel, the rumors were true. In fact, I'm sure I probably fueled them. I was thinking of moving back to town." She took a step closer to him. "But I won't," she said. Pausing, she ran her tongue over her dry lips. "I won't move back here, if you'll promise to stay. Daniel, these people care about you. They love you." Her voice lowered an octave as she added, "They *need* you."

She moved closer. "You may not realize it, but you're an intricate part of this town. You're one of the reasons Fulton is what it is. You can't move away from here."

Taking another step, she was a scant few inches from him. "I promise I'll go. Right after the dinner, I'll pack up my things and go back to Baltimore."

A solitary tear slid silently down her cheek and she dipped her head to hide it. She hated the sound of the words, hated the thought of promising to go back to that lonely apartment in that overcrowded city. But she would. She'd do it for the man she loved. She'd do it for Daniel.

"Savanna."

She started at the sound of his voice. Swiping her hand quickly across her cheek, she lifted her chin and looked into his eyes.

"Savanna, I'm not going anywhere," he said, his tone almost gentle. "I won't lie to you. I did consider moving to Richmond."

His chest expanded as he inhaled, and Savanna had a fleeting thought of how comforting it would be to rest her head there.

"But," he continued, "do you remember the day we painted the room in your house?"

She would never forget the fun she'd had with him that day.

"The day we had ice cream cones on the front porch?" he asked.

She nodded.

"Well, you went on and on about Fulton. You listed the town's attributes as only an out-of-towner could."

Savanna didn't understand why he suddenly looked chagrined.

"I was a little embarrassed," he explained, "that I had forgotten them. All the wonderful things Fulton has to offer, all the great reasons my parents chose to raise their children here, all the amazing qualities that make Fulton the place I want to be in. I left your house that day in a rush, if you remember. And I made a call to Richmond, declining their offer. I came to your house later that night to tell you. But..." He couldn't meet her gaze. "We got...side tracked."

Her breath leaving her in one wild rush, Savanna felt relief flood through her whole body.

Daniel shifted his weight. "So you see, I'm staying in Fulton, after all. My mind is made up. My decision isn't changing. No matter what."

His gaze took on that same unreadable quality she'd come to know so well since returning to town.

"But whether you stay, or whether you go...

that's entirely up to you." His mouth turned up in a dismal grin. "I learned a long time ago that it's wise to let you make up your own mind about those things."

Savanna knew he wasn't making fun of her, he was simply stating a fact, a hard-learned lesson that had caused him a great deal of heartache.

"You know, now that I think about it, maybe we should go back inside." He indicated the hospital with a jerk of his head "Let's clear up this rumor about my leaving town."

As they walked back toward the big glass entry doors in silence, Savanna was acutely aware that Daniel kept a wide margin of space between them.

CHAPTER TEN

———

Savanna's emotions had been flip-flopping for days. She didn't know where she stood. Out in the middle of that dark parking lot nearly two weeks ago, had Daniel been suggesting she stay in Fulton? Or go?

Closing her eyes, she could conjure the sound of his voice, the gentle but firm manner in which he'd assured her that he was staying in town whether she moved back to Fulton or not. But she hadn't been able to decide if his reassurance had been out of some tender feeling he had for her, or if he'd just been kind because he was confronted by a crying female.

And what about their night of love-making? Did he regret it? At first, she'd been sure he had. But after having days and days to think about it, what if he was merely confounded by the whole thing? What if he didn't know what to feel, or what to say, or how to act? One fact remained certain; *she* was completely perplexed by the passionate encounter. How could he feel any different? They needed to talk.

She'd have loved nothing more than to do just that, but the opportunity had never presented itself. The gala dinner had been the sole focus of her attention since the last board meeting. It had begun with a couple of minor snags that she'd have normally described as irritating. However, then the catering company had contacted her with a necessary menu change. The problems snowballed until she was spending every waking moment redirecting, rethinking, and reorganizing. The fact that her reputation rested on the success of this fund-raiser never left her mind for a moment.

Sitting on the edge of her bed, she leaned forward and tucked her toes into the foot of the black stocking. She gently pulled the gossamer fabric up her leg and fastened it with garter hooks.

For important evenings, Savanna always chose stockings over panty hose or even bare legs. The silky sexiness of them were an extravagance that made her feel wonderful, and the lacy garter belt only added to her self-confidence, which was just the thing she needed for a night like tonight.

The much-awaited gala dinner to benefit Fulton General Hospital was less than two hours off. She had been at the country club all day completing a myriad of last-minute tasks, and now, as she thought over the past few weeks, she realized that she'd ended up working harder on this event than she had on any other fund-raising campaign she'd organized.

Savanna slipped on the other silk stocking. After her confrontation with Daniel, she'd felt as though she might drown as she had become engulfed by plans for the dinner. She'd designated who would be in charge of the setting up, decorating, food, entertainment, door prizes, cleaning up and a long tally of other particulars. She had compiled a list of detailed instructions for each volunteer, had personally taken each person to the country club so they could go over their responsibilities, step by painstaking step. Yes,

Savanna had spent what felt like hundreds of hours planning this dinner to perfection.

But every night as she'd crawled, bone weary, between her cool, cotton sheets, Daniel's face would loom in her thoughts and she'd wonder where he was, what he was doing. On the two occasions when she had run into him since the board meeting, he'd pressed her about the details and how things were going until she'd become miffed. Of course she knew he didn't *want* her to fail, but it was pretty clear that he wouldn't be all that surprised if she did. And that hurt. However, both times they'd crossed paths, he had looked at her with an intensity that had sent shivers coursing through her.

As she stepped into her red sequined party dress, she realized that was what was throwing her off. That heated, thoughtful expression in Daniel's eyes. It was keeping her guessing about everything, churning up questions that refused to die.

Did he expect her to leave Fulton after the dinner as she had promised that night in the parking lot? Or was that powerful gaze a silent plea for her to stay? Was he slowly coming to realize that she was devoted to completing her promise of helping Fulton General? Or was merely seeing her a continuing agony for him, an agony of haunting memories of her running away so long ago?

Damn it! She hated that her mind was spinning like this.

The question about their date for tonight had been answered by a quick phone call from him just yesterday morning. As Savanna zipped up her fitted evening dress, she replayed the conversation in her head.

"So, you're still in town," he'd remarked after she'd picked up the receiver.

"Looks like I am," she'd said, confused by the myriad underlying meanings his quip might have held.

He'd hesitated then. "I'm calling to see if we're still on for tomorrow evening."

"I'm game if you are," she'd told him.

She would have liked nothing better than to hear him say he'd been all wrong about her lack of stick-to-it-iveness, but that hadn't happened. In fact, there hadn't been much more to their exchange before he'd suggested an agreed upon time for him to swing by for her.

So here she was, dolling herself up, feeling smug

that, in fulfilling her promise to Daniel, a promise he probably saw as a threat of some sort, to stick around until the dinner was a complete success, she'd somehow proved something. She adjusted the thin strap of her dress and shook her head. How could she feel such love for a man who had so little faith in her? Heaven only knew, but love him she did. With all her heart. Just what she was going to do about that fact was totally beyond her.

Rolling her hair into a neat French twist, she tucked in the ends and secured them with pins. The earrings she wore reflected the light in bright sparkles with each tilt of her head. Finally, she slipped her feet into cherry-red stilettos. The night promised to be clear and hot, much too warm for a wrap. Savanna picked up her handbag and went downstairs to wait for Daniel.

At the bottom step, she heard a small, muffled knock. She followed the sound into the kitchen and pulled open the back door.

"Hi, Jimmy," she said, pushing open the screen. One look at his face had her asking, "What's wrong?"

His gray eyes were huge. "Will you come?"

Savanna bent and looked him in the eye. "What is it, honey?"

"It's Mom. She's got a belly ache."

His face was pale and his bottom lip threatened to tremble.

"Let's go," she said.

Jimmy darted through the green shrubbery hedge that separated her house from the Thompsons'. Savanna cursed her high heels and sequins and hurried around the bushes.

"Sheila?" she called, stepping into the kitchen.

"In here."

Savanna hurried through the dining room where she stumbled upon Amanda. The toddler was naked, except for a fluffy towel, her hair wringing wet. She was quietly singing, "Takin' a baff, it's baff time."

Swooping Amanda up into her arms, Savanna said, "Mmmm. You smell so clean. Where's Mommy, Amanda?"

The little girl wriggled out of her embrace and pointed toward the living room.

"Miss Savanna!" Jimmy called, his voice strained.

Sheila was reclining on the couch, breathing

deeply, eyes closed, her face shining with a thin sheen of perspiration. She was clearly in the middle of a strong contraction.

"Where's your dad?" Savanna asked Jimmy.

"He already left."

"For the country club?"

Jimmy nodded. "He's givin' a 'portant speech."

"I know," she said softly. She couldn't help smiling at the pride in the little boy's voice.

"Sheila, how long have you been having pains?" she asked, dipping into her purse for her cell phone.

A small gasp escaped from Sheila's lips and she exhaled loudly. 'Don't you dare call Jim. I told him to go to the dinner without me," Sheila said. "I haven't been feeling well all day. But I'll be all right."

"I'm not calling Jim. I'm calling an ambulance. The baby's coming, Sheila."

Sheila reached over and touched her son's arm. "Honey, go check on Amanda for me, would you?" Once her son was out of earshot, she firmly said, "No ambulance. It'll scare the kids. Besides it's too early for me to be having this baby. It's a false alarm. Braxton Hicks contractions, they're called.

My body's practicing. It's nothing. I told Jimmy he shouldn't bother you, but he wouldn't listen, the little rascal."

Savanna flipped her phone closed, but couldn't help voicing the concern she felt. "Are you sure? I don't mind taking you."

"No, no," Sheila insisted. "You have a dinner to run tonight. There's no way I'd keep you from the gala. You've worked too hard for this."

Just then she was struck with another wave of pain intense enough to cut her off in mid-sentence. She closed her eyes and concentrated on taking deep, relaxing breaths.

The seconds ticked away anxiously and Savanna's panicky thoughts raced. "Sheila, please..."

Sheila exhaled and looked up at Savanna, a line of beaded sweat across her top lip. "Something's wrong," Sheila said weakly. "The contractions shouldn't be this strong or this close together. "

Savanna jumped to action. "Jimmy," she called out, "bring Amanda here." To Sheila, she said "I'll get her dressed. You're sure you don't want an ambulance?"

Sheila nodded, and murmured, "The kids will

be scared. But if you could take me to the hospital...you wouldn't have to stay. There's an overnight bag in my room at the foot of the bed."

"I'll call the country club," Savanna said, mentally ticking off tasks, "and tell Jim to meet us at the hospital."

A frown bit deep into Sheila's brow. "He's going to be so disappointed. He's been looking forward to tonight. What if this is nothing?"

But Sheila looked like she no longer believed that to be the case

"He'd be more disappointed," Savanna said, helping Sheila out of the chair, "to miss the birth of this baby." Then she shouted, "Jimmy! Bring Amanda here."

"Is this who you're looking for?"

At the sound of Daniel's voice, Savanna swung around and saw him in the doorway with a filthy, squirming Amanda in his arms.

Daniel grinned. "I found this little nudist playing in the flower beds out front."

Jimmy trailed in behind Daniel. "'Manda wouldn't listen to me, Mom."

"Oh, Daniel," Sheila exclaimed. "You're going to get your tux dirty. Put her down."

Savanna thought no man ever looked so good. The cut of the dark dinner jacket hugged his broad chest. The crisp white shirt accentuated his tanned complexion. She tried to tamp down the embers of desire that sparked to life within her. She had too many other things to think about right now, but, Lord, he did look hot.

Daniel focused on her, his brown eyes intent. "What's going on?" he asked.

Savanna tilted her head toward Sheila. "We're having a baby."

"We can't possibly take Amanda to the hospital looking like that," Sheila lamented.

"Can you help me out here, Daniel?" Savanna's tone was pleading.

"Sure," he said. "I'll do anything."

"You take Sheila to the hospital. I'll call Jim to meet you there." Savanna took Amanda from him. "And I'll stay with the kids."

"But your dinner," Sheila said. "They'll need you."

"I've planned everything perfectly," she assured her friend. "I made sure the dinner would go off without a hitch. With or without me."

"You did, huh?"

Daniel's pointed question rubbed her wrong.

"Don't be a snot. It wasn't because I planned on leaving. It was because in my years of putting these functions together, I've learned to expect the unexpected."

"Well, this is as unexpected as it gets." Sheila groaned, wobbling toward the front door. "We have to go. Now."

Savanna shifted Amanda to her other hip. "Jimmy, go get your mom's overnight bag." To Daniel, she said, "I am a little worried about Jim's speech, though."

His dark eyes twinkled as he suggested, "Miz Ida would love to have a captive audience."

"Hmm. Good idea," Savanna said. "I'll tell Jim to give his speech to Ida. With a few adjustments..." her voice trailed as she pulled out her phone.

By the time she'd finished her short conversations, first with Jim, then with Ida, and wrapped the towel around Amanda, she found Daniel outside helping Sheila into the car.

"Buckle up." He slid the seat belt out as far as it would go and handed the metal buckle to Sheila.

Jimmy ran to the car. "Here's the bag."

"Jimmy snot," Amanda said on a giggle.

The slur had the boy grimacing. "Mom!"

"Amanda!" Sheila scolded.

Savanna's mouth twisted with chagrin. "Sorry. That was my fault."

Daniel took the suitcase from Jimmy and pushed it into the back seat. He rounded the car and opened the door, marveling that Savanna didn't seem flustered by this unexpected turn of events.

"Jim's on his way," Savanna said. "And Ida's in control."

He watched her lean through the open passenger window and kiss Sheila on the cheek.

"Good luck," she told her friend. "And don't worry about the kids. They'll be fine."

Daniel wanted to tell her he was sorry that she was missing the dinner she'd worked so hard to put together, but the words snagged in his throat like a fish hook.

"What are you waiting for?" Savanna's deep blue eyes stared into his. "Get her there safely."

"I will."

"I'd better get inside," she said, grinning. "Amanda needs a bath. And Jimmy needs some ice cream, don't you Jimmy?"

Daniel slid behind the wheel and started the

engine. Looking in the rear-view mirror as he drove off, he caught sight of Savanna going up the front porch steps, the slit in the back of her red dress showing a sexy slice of thigh.

When he'd stood in the doorway of Sheila's living room and seen Savanna in that clingy dress, he'd nearly fallen to his knees to thank God she was his date for the evening. The long expanse of lithe leg exposed had caused his heart to thump so hard he'd thought it would burst through his rib cage. His mind had begun to conjure images of them dancing to a slow tune, her body pressed tight to his.

"Daniel!" Sheila shouted.

He slammed his foot on the brake pedal and stopped at the intersection. "Sorry," he muttered.

"Just be careful," she said. Sheila leaned her head against the headrest and closed her eyes. "I can't believe I'm causing Savanna to miss her dinner."

"She didn't seem to mind," he said, turning left and heading into town.

He realized his words were true, and that surprised him. A scowl dug into his brow. First, he'd accused her of not possessing the persevering character it would take to pull off this dinner. And he'd continued to hound her with his distrust. Now that she had shown him just how resolved she was, he found it necessary to attack her again. Why was he surprised by the fact that she didn't mind missing all the accolades that were due her for her hard work, all the praise that would have surely been forthcoming if she'd been present at the gala dinner tonight?

Why, he wondered, did he continue to persist in finding fault in Savanna?

"She's a good person."

Sheila murmured her opinion as though in answer to his silent question. Then she began to breathe deeply, in a way that told Daniel he'd better hurry.

The simple statement Sheila made ate at him. Savanna *was* a good person. She had been six years ago when he'd wanted her for his wife, and she still was now. Her running away from him hadn't changed that.

When Savanna had stood in that parking lot and admitted she wanted to stay in Fulton, and then turned right around and promised to leave if he'd stay, she'd touched a place in him that hadn't seen the light of day in a very long time. Her selflessness had warmed his soul, and the cold, hard iceberg that had been his heart since she had left him six years ago had begun the long process of melting.

He turned on his hazard lights, slowed down, and checked for traffic before cruising through a red light.

He'd spent the past two weeks rethinking the enigma that was Savanna. She had told him she'd be in town for the fund-raising dinner, but his stubbornness had kept him from believing in her. She'd tried time and again to show him how dedicated she was to the hospital's plight. But his injured pride had blinded him to her efforts.

Slowly, over the past days, he'd come to the realization that he needed to be honest with her. At the very least, he must congratulate her on her fund-raising achievements. If the charitable forecasts continued on schedule, Fulton General would be well on its way to running in the black. He knew she deserved a pat on the back.

But if he were to be truly honest with her, he'd have to tell her how he felt. He'd have to tell her...

"Daniel!" Sheila gasped. "Turn here!"

Daniel slowed the car and pulled into the hospital's emergency entrance.

* * *

Putting a mug of water into the microwave oven, Savanna closed the door and pushed the buttons to heat it. She glanced at the clock on Sheila's kitchen wall and thought that, if Ida was keeping to the dinner program, the scheduled speeches should have been over and dinner should have already been served.

A smile tickled across Savanna's mouth as she remembered Miz Ida's self-doubt when the woman found out that she would be in charge. Savanna had gently encouraged her, giving her detailed instructions and telling her where she could find the master list of who was responsible for what. Savanna had assured Ida that she felt everyone was fully prepared and that she was just a phone call away if anything went haywire. Although Ida had called her several times, it was clear that the event was going off as planned.

Savanna's smile widened further as she thought about Jimmy and little Amanda. She'd given Amanda a second bath, which hadn't been an easy task while wearing sequins. Then, after reading the toddler a story, she'd tucked Amanda into bed with a teddy bear. Jimmy had been too worried about his mother to fall asleep, so Savanna simply sat with him. It wasn't long before his eyes began to droop and she tiptoed out of his room.

The microwave beeped, signaling that her water was hot. She dropped a herbal tea bag into the mug to steep, wondering if Daniel would return soon, or stay with Jim until the baby was born. Either way, she hoped she would eventually see him again tonight.

What was she going to do? She wanted to move home to Fulton so badly she could taste it. And she wanted Daniel.

As a rule, confrontation was her forte. It was simply her nature to boldly go after whatever it was she wanted. The tactic was how she'd become a professional success. But the memory of confronting Daniel at the board meeting made her extremely hesitant to admit her feelings to him.

Still, the overwhelming need to know if she and Daniel had a chance refused to go away. She had to find out, one way or the other. So taking a sip from her steaming mug, she devised a plan. A moonlit, romantic plan.

Around ten o'clock that evening, she was sitting on the front porch swing, its chains squeaking a slow, rhythmic tune, when two sets of headlights broke through the darkness. She was happy to see a smiling Jim get out of his car. But the sight of Daniel ambling toward her, still in his tux, had her feeling nervous. Breathless.

"Well?" she asked Jim excitedly. "Do you have a new son, or a new daughter?"

"Danielle Savanna Thompson weighed in at seven pounds, eleven and a half ounces." Jim's mouth split into a proud grin.

"A beautiful baby girl." Daniel thumped the new father on the back.

"Congratulations!" Savanna said, feeling honored that the baby was named after not only herself but Daniel too. "How's Sheila?"

"She's just fine." Jim came up the porch steps. "A little tired, but real happy. She told me to scoot on home so you and Daniel could go to the country club."

"It's only a few minutes past ten." Daniel stared up at her, his hand on the newel post. "We could make it over there in plenty of time for the last dance."

"I'll need to go home and lock up," she said. Savanna descended the steps toward him, calling over her shoulder, "Good night, Jim. And congratulations again."

"Thanks for everything, Savanna," he said.

Daniel took her hand and tucked it in the crook of his arm and they made their way along the sidewalk.

"Daniel," she began haltingly, "would you mind... terribly.. if we didn't go to the country club?"

"No." He shook his head. "But I thought you might like to check on things."

"I've kept in touch with Ida. Everything's going smoothly." She offered him a sheepish little smile. "There's something else I'd rather do."

"Anything," he murmured tenderly. "This is your night."

By then, they had arrived at her house. She turned to face him at the base of the porch steps.

"My night?" she asked.

He nodded, moonlight throwing shadows on the smooth planes of his face. "I want to congratulate you on your success. Both of your fund-raising projects have gone much better than I ever anticipated. I should have said it before but..." He let his voice trail off and looked at the ground. Lifting his gaze, he said, "There's been talk." One corner of his lips quirked up. "A rumor, you might say, that Fulton General should become a client. Of yours, I mean."

She couldn't hide her surprise. The news that the board wanted to hire her took a back seat to his praise. In the weeks she'd been working on the dinner, not once had he complimented her.

"If it's not too far for you to travel," he quickly added.

"Oh, no," she assured him. "I have clients up and down the East Coast." *Besides*, she wanted to add, *if I have my way, I'll be living right here in Fulton.* But for some reason she couldn't utter the words. She still couldn't get over the fact that he'd said something nice about the job she'd done.

"Good." He stepped away from her and tugged at the hem of his dinner jacket. "I'll let the board know you're open to the idea." He cocked his head slightly. "So what was it you wanted to do?"

She felt a devilish anxiety tingle in the pit of her stomach. "Wait right here. I'll only be two seconds."

Dashing into the house and through to the kitchen, she snatched the small transistor radio off the top of the refrigerator and went back outside.

"Let's go," she said, grabbing his hand and propelling him around the side of the house toward the backyard.

"I have something I want to tell you." She felt breathless and excited. She fiddled with the dial until she found a slow, romantic love song. "But first..." She leaned the radio against the tree trunk, stood and kicked off her red shoes. "Will you dance with me?"

Starlight caught the quizzical gleam in Daniel's eye. He seemed too perplexed to reply. Deciding to take his silence as affirmation, Savanna stepped close and his arms closed around her as if it were the most natural thing in the world.

"You want to go under the gazebo?"

From the way his question was expressed, Savanna could tell he felt as jittery as she.

"No," she told him. "Here is fine."

The grass was soft and cool against her stockinged feet, and she felt cocooned in Daniel's arms. He smelled so good; that sensuous scent of sandalwood that always started her nerve endings jangling. His hand enveloped hers in a loose, warm grasp. Slowly they started to sway under the night sky.

The scene was set. The perfect number of stars, the perfect amount of moonlight, everything was perfectly romantic. Now she only had to find the perfect words.

"The six years I was away," she began, "changed me."

She watched his throat muscles tighten as he swallowed.

"I'd agree with that." His voice came out in a husky whisper.

"I've become...self-reliant." She looked up at him through lowered lashes. "Some would even use the word *bold*."

Daniel held back a grin. "I'll agree with that too."

The music ended and they stood facing each other, their gazes locked. A flash of self-consciousness ripped through her and she reached up to tuck back the curly tendrils of her hair that had escaped from the pins, but Daniel caught her wrist in his fingers.

"Don't," he whispered. "It's perfect just the way it is."

She smiled. Another slow tune began to drift on the warm evening air and they once again began to move to the alluring rhythm.

Dancing in lazy circles, enveloped by Daniel's strong arms, Savanna knew without a doubt that she wanted this man to know all that was in her heart. There could be no easy way to tell him. If he wasn't able to overcome the distrust he felt, then she'd have to learn to live with that.

"Daniel," she whispered, "I want you."

He stopped dancing and stood motionless, his arms still around her, his questioning eyes fastened on hers.

"I want you," she repeated louder. "I want to move back to Fulton, and I want you in my life. I love you, Daniel."

It was obvious that her revelations stunned him.

She rushed on, "I made a mistake six years ago..."

He cut her off by lifting his hand and placing a finger gently against her lips.

Shaking his head, he replied, "Don't ever say that. Don't ever call it a mistake."

Daniel caressed her cheek and Savanna leaned into it, closing her eyes and reveling in the feel of his touch. Then he rubbed the pad of his thumb over her bottom lip.

"If you hadn't left," he said, "you wouldn't be the person you are now. You needed to go. You had to go. I didn't understand that before. But I do now."

She looked into his eyes and her heart swelled with love.

"I tried so hard to prove myself."

Again he stopped her words with gentle fingers.

"You did," he said. "Although you shouldn't have had to, you did prove yourself. You proved a lot of things, but I was too damned pigheaded to realize."

She reached up and took his hand in hers. And after kissing the fingertips resting against her lips, she pulled them away to grin and say, "I'd agree with that."

He chuckled, a rich, sexy sound emanating from deep in his chest.

"But," she whispered, her gaze taking on an utter seriousness, "that doesn't make me want you any less."

"I want you too," he said. "I've wanted you since the day you arrived back in town." He pulled her even tighter against him, his desire laid bare by his lowered eyelids, his burning gaze, his gravelly sigh. "I love you. I don't think I ever stopped."

The breath she expelled overflowed with relief. "I was so sure you regretted sleeping with me."

"Not for a second." He cupped her jaw in the palm of his hand and covered her mouth with his. His lips were warm and moist, and they kindled in Savanna a passion that overwhelmed her with its intensity. Her heartbeat quickened and, without thought, without excuses, she gave in to the sensual aura encircling them. With an excruciating slowness that bordered on erotic, she traced the tip of her tongue across his hot, silken lips. It was all the invitation Daniel needed.

Lost in his hungry kiss, Savanna vaguely discerned the sound of ragged breathing and couldn't tell if it was Daniel's or her own. The sudden urge to be closer to him compelled her to blindly fumble for the button of his suit jacket. Once she'd unfastened it, she slid her arms under the satiny lining and around his waist. The taste of his lips on hers, the feel of his touch on her skin, even the scent of him, made her dizzy with pleasure, delirious with happiness.

Finally she drew back, her eyes growing misty

as she looked at him. "Once, I ran away from the perfect man." She rested her forehead lightly against his chin, astonished by the sheer perfection of being in his arms.

She lifted her gaze to his. Her voice grew sultry as she reached up and slid her hand behind his neck to pull him closer. "And now that I've found him again, I never want to let him go."

She kissed him then, under a velvet black sky filled with twinkling stars. And as Savanna was surrounded by the Southern summer night, enveloped by the heady scent of lilacs and the warmth of Daniel's love, she knew she was home.

A Note From the Author

Hello!

I hope you enjoyed Return of the Runaway Bride. I wrote the book after overhearing a conversation between a mother and daughter in an elevator at a local department store. The women had just picked up a bridal gown and the daughter said to her mom, "I just don't think I can go through with this." Her anguish touched me to the core, and before I knew it, a story began to take shape.

If you enjoyed the book, please consider taking a moment to write a review. Good reviews help new readers find my books. Consider telling your romance-reading friends about it; word of mouth recommendations are the best way for me to find new readers. I really appreciate your help.

For more information about me and the books I've written, visit my website at:

www.DonnaFasano.com

I love to hear from readers!

My best to you.

Donna Fasano

About the author

Donna Fasano is a USA TODAY Bestselling Author whose books have sold nearly 4 million copies worldwide and have been translated into two dozen languages. She lives on Maryland's Eastern Shore with her husband and Roo, their twelve-year-old Australian cattle dog mix.

Other Books by Donna Fasano

Following His Heart, Ocean City Boardwalk
Series, Book 1
Two Hearts In Winter, Ocean City Boardwalk
Series, Book 2
Wild Hearts of Summer, Ocean City Boardwalk
Series, Book 3
An Almost Perfect Christmas, Ocean City
Boardwalk Series, Book 4
*Grown-Up Christmas List, Ocean
CityBoardwalk Series, Book 5*
The Wedding Planner's Son, Ocean City
Boardwalk Series, Book 6
Reclaim My Heart
The Merry-Go-Round
Her Fake Romance

The Single Daddy Club Series: Derrick, Book 1
The Single Daddy Club Series: Jason, Book 2
The Single Daddy Club Series: Reece, Book 3
Take Me, I'm Yours
His Wife for a While
An Accidental Family
Mountain Laurel
and others

Non-fiction Books
Prayer of Quiet
Favorite Christmas Cookies
Recipes of Love
Guy Food